BORN IN A BLACK CAB

Born in a Black Cab
An anthology of stories
ISBN: 978-1-913781-07-1

Published by CAAB Publishing Ltd (Reg no 12484492)

C . A . A . B
PUBLISHING

Serenity House, Foxbridge drive, Chichester, UK
www.caabpublishing.co.uk

First Published 2021
Printed in the UK

British Library Cataloguing in Publication data available

BORN IN A BLACK CAB
VARIOUS ARTISTS

Here you will find a collection of tales, all starting life in a black cab. Some may thrill you, some may scare, but all will entertain.

So, hail that taxi, climb inside and join us as we scream and pant our way to birthing a new creation. Witness the delivery and don't worry, the meter isn't running so enjoy the ride.

CONTENTS

WHEN SORRY IS NO LONGER ENOUGH
BY PAUL RHODES

The protesters' contorted faces squashed against the taxi's windows as the security agents fought them back with baton strikes. The taxi inched forward through the hostile crowd, towards the open gates of the Blue Sky Institute. Heavy fists hammered at the polished black body of the vehicle with resounding thuds.

"That's why they sent me and not one of those new driverless models," the cabbie said. "A driverless taxi would shut down with all that banging. It'd think it'd been in an accident."

He glanced into his rear-view mirror at the well-dressed couple.

"For what it's worth, I think you're doing the right thing," he said. "It can't be easy."

"Thank you," said Mrs Copeland, squeezing her husband's hand.

The taxi's thick steel chassis and layered acoustic glass smothered the crowd's jeers to a low rumble as they crawled through to the driveway.

The security guards, clad in black paramilitary body armour, sprayed the protesters with gas while the heavy gates began to close behind them.

"Don't worry, I know where I'm going," the cabbie said, as he accelerated up the driveway and around the low sprawling glass building.

Rows of newly planted silver birch trees, their trunks protected by clear plastic tubes, stretched back from the driveway. Beyond them, an already established forest of oak.

Mrs Copeland breathed a long sigh of relief as the gates and the protesters with their crudely constructed placards disappeared from view. Without all that chaos, you could have been anywhere. The Blue Sky Institute looked to be nothing more than a modern hotel, situated peacefully in the beautiful Kent countryside.

"I'll wait for you here," the cabbie said, pulling the taxi up to the entrance. "You've got me for the day so there's no need to hurry."

"We won't be long," Mr Copeland said, straightening his tie in the rear-view. "Dragging it out's not going to help anyone."

#

"Was I in an accident?" Reggie mumbled.

He blinked, struggling to focus through the washed-out blur.

An open door gave way to a shock of white light. Shapes formed and dissolved away. Pulsing around him in a mash of grey and blue.

"Who's there?" Reggie asked, trying to raise his leaden shoulders.

He couldn't move.

A thick buckled belt ran across the bedsheets, pinning his hips. Tight Velcro straps scratched at his wrists and ankles.

"We'll give you a few minutes together once he's fully awake," a voice said. "You should expect some hostility. Patients generally become very agitated before this type of procedure."

"My husband and I are prepared for that, Doctor," a woman's voice replied. "Your ante-fatal team have been incredibly supportive."

Craning his neck, Reggie watched as figures began to materialise around him. Clothed in ocean-coloured medical scrubs with matching masks, they filled the tiny room. One of them held a navy suit-bag by its hanger. The name of the designer splayed across it in gold italic lettering.

"Did you bring shoes for him too, Mrs Copeland?" a nurse asked.

"Oh God, I've left them in the taxi," Mrs Copeland answered. "It was all those protesters when we pulled up. I wasn't expecting so many."

"Mum, is that you?" Reggie called out.

8

"There's no hurry," the nurse said, placing her hand on Mrs Copeland's arm. "You can give them to me after the procedure."

"I'll go and get his shoes," Mr Copeland said. "I'll be glad to get this bloody mask off. I don't know why you're making us wear them, given the circumstances."

"Henry, please," Mrs. Copeland said.

"Dad?" Reggie shouted. "Dad, what's going on?"

A pair of spectacled grey eyes peered down at Reggie. The lower half of the face obscured by a surgical mask.

"Reggie Copeland," the voice behind the mask said. "My name is Dr Bryce. I will be conducting your procedure today, assisted by Drs Thompson and Rodriguez."

"Hello," Dr Thompson and Dr Rodriguez said in unison, appearing on either side of Dr Bryce.

"Mum?" Reggie tried again. "Mum, what's happening?"

"I'm going to clear the room now," Dr Bryce said. "So you can spend a few moments with your parents before we take you down to surgery."

"Surgery?" Reggie said. "I'm not sick."

"Well, that's a matter of opinion," Dr Rodriguez said.

"If you could wait outside the door for me please, gentlemen," Dr Bryce said to Dr Thompson and Dr Rodriguez. "I'll give you a shout when it's time for the gas."

"Gas, what gas?" Reggie asked as they left the room.

"Sevoflurane," Dr Thompson called back from the corridor.

"Dr Thompson's a wonderful anaesthetist, Reggie," Dr Bryce said. "You're in very safe hands."

There was no other furniture in the room. No equipment. A sole burst of colour came from a picture on the wall at the foot of Reggie's bed. A blazing sun setting on a cornfield painted in oil. Thick swathes of red, black, and gold.

"That was made by one of our patients," Dr Bryce said proudly. "Her parents gifted it as a thank you."

Reggie squirmed beneath the weight of the leather strap. His dark eyes inscrutable while his racing mind searched for an out.

"Look Reggie, there's no easy way of saying this," Dr Bryce said, pushing his wire-framed glasses back from the tip of his nose.

"Your parents have exercised their right to terminate you. As per the Reproductive Rights Extended Ownership Act of 2024."

"What?" Reggie screamed, writhing violently against the taut restraints. "You can't!"

Dr Bryce stared blankly at his patient's reddening face. There was no fear registering in the boy's wild eyes. Just rage.

"Take a breath, Reggie," Dr Bryce said. "Accept what I'm saying."

"Eat shit," Reggie snarled, spitting a thick spray of phlegm across Dr Bryce's face.

"Reggie!" Mrs Copeland cried out.

"It's quite alright, Mrs Copeland. *That's* why we wear masks," Dr Bryce said, wiping the spittle from his forehead with the back of a latex-gloved hand.

"As I was saying, Reggie," Dr Bryce continued. "Your parents have an absolute right of ownership over you until your 18th birthday and..."

"But that's next month!"

"Which is why we need to act now," Dr Bryce said. "As an adult, you'd have the right to appeal before an involuntary euthanasia panel, have your case heard at the Supreme Court... It could get very ugly for your parents, Reggie. Not to mention costly."

"We didn't reach this decision lightly," Mrs Copeland said, leaning over the bed so Reggie could see her. "There's been months of consultation."

"Without me?!?"

"Be reasonable, Reggie," Dr Bryce said. "We couldn't expect you to discuss your own termination objectively, could we?"

"Listen to what Dr Bryce is telling you, son," Mr Copeland said. "It's for the best."

"For who?" Reggie hissed. "You're having me executed!"

"Now, that's not fair," Dr Bryce said, shaking his head. "The Blue Sky Institute is a professional medical facility. We pride ourselves on…"

"Help me!" Reggie shrieked, thrashing against his shackles.

"The least you could do is go quietly, son," Mr Copeland said. "After everything you've put us through."

"But terminations are for killers and paedophiles," Reggie said. "I've done nothing like that!"

"Think of it as future-proofing." Dr Bryce said.

"No, this isn't happening," Reggie said. "You're just trying to scare me. You couldn't possibly…"

"Dr Bryce," Mrs Copeland asked. "Could we have a moment alone with our son?"

"Of course," he replied. "I'll be just outside the door for any technical questions."

Dr Bryce left the room, and Mrs Copeland took his place at the head of the bed. Looking sadly at Reggie, she ran her hand through his thick brown curls.

"They've been watching you, Reggie," Mrs Copeland said, pulling her mask down and resting it under her chin.

"What do you mean?"

"Miss Fields, the tutor you've been seeing to get your grades up…" Mrs Copeland continued.

"What about her?"

"She's a forensic psychiatrist, Reggie," Mrs Copeland said. "She's been assessing your behaviour."

Mrs Copeland's hands trembled as she fussed with her son's hair. The wild curls he'd inherited from her. The dark, searching eyes and pinched features were her husband's.

"You've got a neurodevelopmental disorder, Reggie," Mrs Copeland said. "You've been red-flagged."

She sighed. A thick tear ran down her cheek and dropped silently onto Reggie's pillow.

"You're doing great, love," Mr Copeland said, rubbing his wife's back.

"Please, Mum. I can change," Reggie said, looking up at her. "Don't do this."

"You can't change, Reggie," Mrs Copeland replied. "We've seen the predictive metrics. You're only going to get worse."

"No, you can't let them do this," Reggie pleaded. "Dad, say something!"

"You're wired wrong, son," Mr Copeland said quietly. "Simple as that."

"This can't still be about the cat?" Reggie said. "I was nine. I didn't know..."

"That's just it, you should have known," Mrs Copeland said. "What you did to her beautiful tail... And with my pruning secateurs too!"

Mr Copeland produced a neatly folded handkerchief from his pocket and handed it to his wife.

"It's not just the cat, son," Mr Copeland said, pulling down his mask. "You've made our lives unbearable. We can't go anywhere without someone telling us that you've damaged their property or hurt their children..."

"When I think about what you put that poor Hazel through," Mrs Copeland said, dabbing at her tears with the handkerchief. "Following her, sending those awful letters. The dead animals you left on her doorstep..."

"That was *her* fault," Reggie said. "Mum, please... I'm still your little boy."

12

"Enough," Mr Copeland said. "We're not here for a discussion, Reggie. Your mother and I came to say goodbye."

The family of three were silent for a moment, looking at one another as if for the first time.

"What if I just leave?" Reggie asked. "Give me some money and I'll disappear. You'll never hear from me again."

"No, Reggie," Mrs Copeland said firmly. "This has gone on long enough. Miss Fields has made it very clear that you've been manipulating us. That you enjoy all the pain you cause."

"*Dr Fields'* research has shown," said Dr Bryce, re-entering the room, "that it's highly likely your sociopathic tendencies will manifest into something far more dangerous."

"You rotten bastards!" Reggie screamed. "You're murdering your only child!"

Mrs Copeland sighed and turned to Dr Bryce.

"We're ready, Dr Bryce," she said.

"Dr Rodriguez! Dr Thompson!" Dr Bryce called out to the corridor.

Dr Rodriguez and Dr Thompson quickly joined them in the room. Dr Thompson dragging a tall black canister mounted on a hand-truck. A transparent mask attached to a long rubber hose swung freely from the tap.

"No, you can't!" Reggie screeched. "Mummy, please!"

Dr Rodriquez wrapped his hands across Reggie's forehead, interlocking his fingers. Dr Bryce struggling to hold Reggie's chin steady as he squirmed and shrieked.

"Please, stop! I can change, I promise… I'll be a good boy!"

"Okay Reggie, count backwards from 10 with me," Dr Thompson said flatly, forcing the mask over Reggie's mouth and nose.

"Nooooooooooooooo!" Reggie wailed.

"Come on, Reggie," Dr Thompson said. "10."

"9."

"We'll always love you, Reggie," Mrs Copeland said

"8."

"I hate you!" Reggie gasped.

"7."

"That's it, Reggie," Dr Bryce said, tightening his grip. "Deep breaths."

"6."

"We didn't want this, son." Mr Copeland said. "We tried everything."

"5."

"Fuuuuuuuucccccccckkkkkkkkkyyyyyyyyyooooooooouuuuuu!" Reggie gurgled.

"4."

"Oh Reggie," Mrs Copeland said.

"3… 2… That's it," Dr Thompson said. "He's under."

Mrs Copeland slumped across Reggie's legs, sobbing gently into the bedsheets. Mr Copeland stood in silence behind her, his head bowed.

"You are entitled to view the final procedure," Dr Bryce said to Mr and Mrs Copeland. "But I must warn you, the effects of the pancuronium bromide injection can be unpleasant to watch."

"Goodbye, Reggie," Mrs Copeland said, laying her hand on her son's chest, watching it rise and fall with each quiet breath.

"We had such high hopes for you, son," Mr Copeland whispered. Placing his hand on top of hers.

AUTHOR BIO – PAUL RHODES

Factory worker, diplomat, immigration officer, and deckhand are some of the more polite things Paul Rhodes has been called.

Now he's trying to hoodwink people into calling him a writer.

His stories have been published by FTB Press.

He lives in Faversham, England with Faye, Dylan, and Dookie.

WHERE IT ALL BEGAN
BY E. BUNGLE

My story starts, as many great stories do. In a black cab. But I will get to that in a minute for this isn't my story this is the story about my parents and how they met, and their story starts in a different way altogether. It starts with a phone call.

Ring, Ring

"Hello," she answered sleepily as the last vestiges of the dream she had been having slowly disappeared from her memory. It had been a good dream, she thought, but already it was becoming cloudy as the dreams of the night before do in the moments after waking. There was a lot of static, so it took a few seconds for her to realise what had been said on the other end of the phone.

"Hi, is Bob there?" the man's voice on the other side of the phone replied as the static cleared.

"Sorry, what?" she replied, trying to bring her focus completely awake to concentrate on what was going on.

"Is Bob there?" the voice repeated. "It's Andrew, his friend from college."

The lady blinked back the tiredness from her eyes and focused once more. "Bob?" she questioned. "There's no Bob here at the moment."

She quickly chided herself on her clumsy response. "That is to say, there is never a Bob here … I mean, No Bob lives here, there may well have been a Bob here once or twice before but not on any consistent basis, at least that is to say not on any consistent basis since I have been living here." She stopped, flustered, and composed herself. "I'm sorry." She restarted. "I think you have the wrong number." On the other end of the line, Andrew burst into laughing a thick happy laugh that was so infectious that she started to laugh too.

"Well, I am very sorry to have bothered you," he chuckled. "But that has to be the most convoluted way to say wrong number I have ever heard."

"Don't be mean," she chided him but without upset.

"I'm sorry, and I don't mean to be mean. In fact, you have really made my day. Hey what's your name?" he asked.

"I'm not just going to give my name to a random man on the phone, that's for sure," she replied.

"After that little dialogue, I don't think I am the one you should be calling random," he retorted. "Anyway, you know my name, It's Andrew. And you know that I went to college with Bob, even if you don't know who Bob is … and I guess that you know that my good friend Bob doesn't like me enough to update me when he is changing his number, although maybe that doesn't work in my favour."

She laughed at his self-deprecation "Nice to meet you Andrew, unliked friend of Bob, my name is Sasha."

"And it's nice to meet you too Sasha."

She could tell he was smiling as he spoke, and despite the strange circumstances of their meeting, she realised she was beaming as well.

"Anyway, I am very sorry to have disturbed you, Sasha, I will let you get back to sleep, and I am going to try and find someone else to tell my exciting news to as my former best friend clearly no longer cares."

"WAIT," she blurted, a little too vociferously. "I mean, what is your exciting news? After all, you woke me up. The least you can do is tell me what all the fuss is about." She wasn't sure why she had been so desperate for him to stay on the line, but she knew she definitely didn't want him to go.

* * *

"What the hell were you thinking?"

Sasha had just told her best friend Andrea about her telephone conversation, and she wasn't impressed. Sasha looked around the coffee shop embarrassed by her friend's outburst, although no one was paying them any attention at all. "Shhh… not so loud." She complained. "He was nice, we spoke for hours, he made me laugh. I haven't laughed for a long time."

"I understand that, but do you really think after one phone call you should ask him to move in with you?"

"I didn't ask him to move in with me," she scoffed. "I said that when he is visiting next month, he could stay with me if he doesn't manage to find his friend."

"Someone, you don't know. In your house. Still sounds crazy to me." Andrea said unimpressed.

"Anyway, he said he was going to stay in a hotel, but that he wanted to meet up in person. And anyway, I will know him by then as he said he was going to call me again later."

"Someone you have spoken to a couple of times on the phone does not count as someone you know," Andrea sighed. "Look Sash, I am just worried about you and want you to be safe."

"I know, and I am grateful." She placed her hand on her friend's arm. "I promise you, when I meet up with him, I will do it in a public place, and if it makes you feel better, you can be sitting off to the side to check up on him." She smiled at her friend and lifted her coffee cup. "Here's to meeting the first decent man since I moved to this city, even if he comes from the other side of the world."

* * *

"I can't believe we are going to be seeing each other soon," Sasha said as she laid on her bed speaking to Andrew on the phone. "It feels like only yesterday that you said you were coming next month, and now it is only two days away."

"I'm excited to see you too," Andrew said on the other end of the phone. "I have been thinking about this moment for what feels like forever. I can't wait to hold you in my arms and feel your body against mine. Speaking on the phone every day has been wonderful, but there is so much more I want to do with you."

18

"What time do you land?" she asked, "I want to make sure I am at the airport in plenty of time. I hope you look like the photo you sent or else I will never recognize you. Should I wear a flower or something, so you know it is me?"

"No need, as long as you look like the photo you sent me then I can't believe that there will be anyone else in the whole country as beautiful as you."

"Stop it, you get so corny," she said whilst feeling her smile grow bigger than ever. "I don't need to be the most attractive, just as long as you are pleased with me."

"I can't think of anyone I have ever been more pleased with, that I have ever known, and when I can finally hold your hand and kiss your lips, there is no way that will be any less pleasing. But my darling, that time is upon us now, I need to head to the airport so I will be with you as soon as I can. And it must be very late for you now. Get some sleep, I don't want you to be tired when I get there."

"Good night or I guess good afternoon for you. Have a safe flight and we can discuss how tired I am when you get here," she paused, "in this bed beside me."

"Ok, stop," he replied, "or I will not be able to tear myself away and I will miss my flight. Sleep well, my darling."

Sasha hung up the phone and laid back, buzzing with anticipation at seeing him the next day, she was so excited she doubted she would ever get to sleep, and yet within seconds she was drifting off to sleep and once again entering the dream world. In her dream, Andrew arrived, and she pulled him into her bed and started to eagerly undress him. He pushed her back onto the bed and ripped her pyjama top open in one movement, desperate to get his hands on her body. She pulled her pyjamas trousers down as she hooked him with her legs to pull him closer to her. Desperate to feel his body against hers. They started to make love in the dream, and she could feel him inside her and in her ecstasy, she felt like they were starting to become one person. She opened her eyes to look at her lover, but it was no longer Andrew that she saw, it was a beast. He was twice the size of the man he had been, and his eyes glowed red like the sun as he continued to penetrate her. She screamed and pushed him off and suddenly awoke sweating and panting heavily. But it had just been a dream. She raised herself up from the bed and looked at her body. Her pyjama top was ripped and all the buttons, as well as her trousers, were missing. Her breasts were sore and looking at them she saw scratch marks all across her body, and it seemed like her stomach was swelling up as if her whole abdomen was a giant lump.

"But it was just a dream, right?" she thought aloud. She tried to stand, but a sudden pain made her curl over in pain. With the pain coursing through her body, she pulled on a coat and pair of trousers. Then leaning against the wall for support she forced herself along the hallway and into the street.

"TAXI," she screamed in pain, as the black cab drove down the street. "TAXI."

And she collapsed to the floor. The driver of the cab pulled up and rushed to her side. "Are you ok?" he asked, looking at her dishevelled appearance.

"I think I need a hospital," she replied. "Something's wrong."

He helped her to her feet and carefully across to his cab. "Just hold on," he said, "I'll get you to the hospital, your baby will be fine."

She was about to object that she wasn't pregnant, but the pain forced her to just hold her stomach, which seemed to be swelling by the second as pain repeatedly coursed through her body. Meaning it was all she could do not to scream as she was placed into the back of the cab and the driver resumed his place at the front.

"We'll be at the hospital in no time." The cab driver said as he pulled urgently away. As he drove, he reached down and switched on the radio as if that would in any way help take her mind off the pain.

The radio crackled as the song it was playing descended into static, and then it seemed to clear. "Sasha," the voice came through the radio.

"Andrew?" she asked, shocked.

20

"Yes, my darling. It is me," he replied.

"What is happening? How are you on the radio?" She struggled to understand what was going on. "I'm in so much pain."

The cab driver continued driving as if he couldn't hear the conversation, but every few seconds would curse as his progress was held up by another road user.

"Don't worry my darling." Andrew's soothing voice came to her over the radio. "Everything is ok."

"Why aren't you here, I need help," she responded. "Something is wrong with me, I'm scared."

"Don't be scared," he replied. "Everything is going to be alright." As he spoke, she could feel the pain subsiding and the fear starting to leave her body. "You are going to have a baby, my baby."

"What?" she exclaimed quietly, confused. "But how, we have never even met."

"But we did," he soothed. "You see, I am not what you think, I don't come from this world."

"What?" she said, but in a whisper.

"I come from another dimension, I came to you through the radio waves of your phone, but I can never truly enter your world, only my essence can exist there, in dreams, in your dreams."

"What?" she repeated in shock.

"I'm sorry. I was never going to come as I can't live in your dimension." He paused, "but our son can, he can live in your world. He will have a human body but will be of my kind. Through him, a hybrid shall rise that will dominate mankind, and it is all thanks to you."

Sasha sat in the back of the cab and felt herself start to fall, as if the whole world was rushing away from her at high speed. She saw the lights of the hospital as the cab pulled up outside. She heard the driver shouting as he got out and felt a breeze as the door opened. She saw herself being laid on the floor of the cab, as a doctor started to examine her, but she felt like it was happening to someone else.

"It's too late to move her." She heard the doctor say from a distance. "The baby's coming here. Well, at least the child will always have a story to tell, fancy being born in a black cab."

AUTHOR BIO — E. BUNGLE

E. Bungle is a writer of fantasy. In his younger days, he worked for Penguin books and padded out his book collection with their production line rejects. He has been working on his first novel for many years and he hopes that one day he will stop editing it, send it out into the world, and get it rejected by as many agents and publishers as possible. E. Bungle enjoys archery, comedy movies, and a good glass of wine, he also enjoys reading Bernard Cornwell and Terry Pratchett when he gets five minutes peace.

THE FRIENDS YOU MAKE ON HOLIDAY
BY DALE PARNELL

"Where to, pal?"

"The hotel...Alexander," Dominic replied, checking his booking information one final time.

"Right you are," the cab driver replied, clicking on the indicator as he watched in his mirrors for a space in the steady stream of early morning traffic.

Growing tired of waiting, the cab suddenly lurched out into the road, eliciting a chorus of angry horns, and yet the cab driver leaned an arm out of his window and waved good-naturedly; as if thanking an old friend for letting him out. Dominic slid across the smooth, leather seat, grasping for the handle above the door, and as the cab corrected and began driving straight, he yanked the seatbelt free and clipped it in place across his body. The cab quickly settled into a stop/start routine as they pulled away from the airport, and Dominic felt his initial panic ease. The roads were busy, but here, nestled inside his own little pocket of quiet, away from the chaos that had been the airport arrival lounge, Dominic finally allowed himself a private smile.

He had done it.

First thing on the list; ride in a genuine black cab.

For Dominic, it was as English as Buckingham Palace and Shakespeare; bettered only by the authentic double-decker buses he had seen in films as a kid. He glanced up and down the road, looking for the iconic red shape, and was slightly disappointed not to see any, but then he figured they must operate more in the centre of the city.

"Business or pleasure then pal?" asked the cab driver, breaking the silence after a few minutes.

"Pardon?" Dominic replied, unsure what he was referring to.

"Are you here for business, or on holiday like?" the cab driver clarified.

"Oh, right. Yes, holiday. It's my first time in the U.K."

"Well then, welcome to our sceptred isle," the cab driver said, winking in his rear-view mirror. "Staying long?"

"Two weeks," Dominic replied. "A few days here in London, then over to Canterbury, Oxford, the Lake District, then Edinburgh."

The cab driver whistled appreciatively. "That's quite a tour," he said. "I always say I should get out and see more of the country myself."

"Oh?" Dominic said. "Have you lived here long?"

"No, not long," muttered the cab driver, as if totting up the years in his mind for the first time, "two, maybe, three thousand years."

Dominic laughed nervously, trying to remain polite. His friends had warned him that the British have a strange sense of humour, and his immediate feeling was that the cab driver was 'taking the piss', an activity he had been led to believe came as natural as breathing for most British people.

"No, tell a lie," the cab driver corrected, looking at Dominic again through his rear-view mirror. "It's only been one thousand-nine hundred. Isn't it funny how time flies?"

"Yes," murmured Dominic, deciding that he didn't actually like being made to play the part of the gullible tourist.

The traffic had thinned a little, and the cab picked up some speed, joining the motorway heading for the centre of the city.

"Of course, all this is relatively new," the cab driver said, once again breaking the silence. "I remember when it was thick forests, far as you could see."

"Hmm," Dominic sounded, not wanting to take the bait.

The cab driver grinned, a wide, devilish smirk that spread across his whole face, making his eyes glint in the low sunlight. "You don't believe me, do you?"

"No, I get it," Dominic replied, trying to sound good-natured. "I'm sure everyone loves to tease the stupid American tourists."

"I would never accuse anyone of being stupid, Sir," the cab driver said, taking his hands off the steering wheel and turning around bodily to look at Dominic through the Perspex partition screen.

"The road, the road!" Dominic screeched, watching in terror as the cab chased up behind a huge truck.

"Huh?" the cab driver said absent-mindedly, glancing over his shoulder.

The cab came within a few feet of the rear of the truck, and then smoothly glided into the right-hand lane to overtake, easing back in front of the truck, and continuing on its way, all without the cab driver touching a single control.

"How did you…?" Dominic stuttered, slack jawed. He had read something a year or so ago about self-drive technology being developed, but it was still at least ten years away from being on the roads, and nothing about the plain-looking console at the front of the cab indicated that it had been upgraded with any kind of computerised system.

"Oh, she knows where she's going," the cab driver replied, as calmly and plainly as if he were confirming the correct time for you.

"She?" Dominic asked, looking around the cab as if he would find some previously hidden clue as to what the driver was talking about.

"You know, I never did give her a name, isn't that funny?" the cab driver remarked, tenderly stroking the worn leather of his seat.

The cab driver looked up again, seeing Dominic's stunned, confused face staring back. "I'm so sorry, where are my manners? My name's Famine pleased to meet you," he said, extending a wiry, wrinkled hand through the hatch in the middle of the Perspex screen.

***

"Famine? As in… Famine?" Dominic said stupidly, taking the driver's offered hand on autopilot.

"That's right," Famine replied, smiling warmly. "Four horsemen, end of days. And you are?"

It took a moment for Dominic to remember his own name, and he shook his head to try and dislodge the confusion he felt, as if it were a wet towel wrapped around his skull. "What? Yes, Dominic. Fairweather. Dominic Fairweather."

"Pleasure to make you acquaintance, Dom," Famine replied cheerily.

"So, you're actually trying to tell me that you're *the* Famine, from The Bible?" Dominic asked, finally pulling himself together a little.

"Yes," replied Famine, somewhat distractedly. "Look, do you mind?" he asked, nodding to the back seat beside Dominic.

Dominic was about to ask what he meant when he felt the air in the cab whirl around him, and as suddenly as blinking, Famine was no longer sat in the driver's seat and was instead sat beside him in the back of the taxi, his legs stretched out before him, seemingly enjoying the extra space. Dominic screamed. He wished it had been a strong, manly scream, the scream of a warrior about to go into battle, but in truth, it was a child's scream, high pitched and shrill, the kind of scream that says, 'the bogeyman is coming to get me, and I won't stop screaming until my mother picks me up and tells me everything is going to be okay'.

"Whoa," said Famine, holding his hands out pleadingly, "sorry about that, didn't mean to make you wet your nappy!"

The insult worked as well as a slap to the face, and Dominic fell silent, staring wide-eyed at the man who had moments ago magically transported himself from the front seat to the back without so much as an 'Abracadabra!'.

It took a further moment for Dominic to realise that if the driver was sat next to him, then that meant… He turned to the front, staring out of the windscreen as the cab continued to weave in and out of traffic, the steering wheel spinning one way then the other, even managing to click on the turning signal for each overtake.

"Told you she was fine," Famine said proudly.

Dominic turned back to face him. "What are you doing here?" he asked, stupefied.

"Well, I thought there'd be more leg room, you know, space for a proper chat and all that," Famine replied.

"Not *here*, here," Dominic replied, exasperated. "I mean, here, on Earth, now? Is this it, the end times?" he added nervously.

Famine laughed, his tone jovial rather than mocking. "No, of course not. Think of it like a holiday. You have your holidays, to get away from work, don't you? Well, I did the same, sort of."

"You're on holiday?" Dominic asked slowly. "For nineteen hundred years?"

"Yeah, well, taking into account the time I spent on the job beforehand, you could call this a weekend break!" Famine said, chuckling to himself.

"And you're driving a cab?" Dominic said, looking about the taxi.

"I had to bring her with me."

"Who?" asked Dominic.

Famine puffed his chest out theatrically, and when he spoke, his voice was that of a hurricane, vast and huge and terrible. "I looked, and behold, a black horse; and he who sat on it carried mighty scales in his hand, and all the world wept."

Famine eased back into the leather seat, flicking his eyebrows up at Dominic, clearly used to a more appreciative audience.

"I... I..." Dominic stuttered, eyes wide and blinking, a rabbit staring down a shotgun barrel.

Famine suddenly roared with laughter, his body bent double, and he slapped Dominic's leg as if they were old mates.

Dominic looked down at Famine, then up to the road, the cab still travelling along merrily. He turned to stare out of the side windows, seeing drivers and passengers in the cars they passed, yet not one seemed to be reacting to a driverless black cab tearing down the motorway on a sunny Monday morning in mid-July. He'd heard of the stiff-upper-lip, but this was ridiculous. No. It was too much. Dominic had gone to Sunday school as a kid, he'd read bits and pieces of The Bible, and whilst he didn't necessarily believe all of it, he knew the difference between a miracle and a huckster.

"No, I'm not buying it," he said uncertainly. "You're having me on! And the cab, someone's just steering it on remote control." He started scanning the road around the cab, looking for another car nearby that had probably been trailing them since the airport. It was just a con or a reality show, or maybe the cabbie was just plain crazy.

Famine sat upright, his laughter melting away, and he looked on Dominic with something approaching pity.

"Dom, Dom. Listen. It's not a joke, it's not a con. I just…" Famine trailed off, unsure of his next words. "You know what? I just wanted to tell someone. I've been down here, on my own, for so long, and sometimes you just want to be upfront with someone. Do you know what I mean?"

"Prove it," said Dominic, turning to face him.

"Sorry pal?"

"Prove that you're really Famine," Dominic said more firmly.

"You don't want me to do that," said Famine, his voice suddenly very serious.

"I do! If you're really him, you can prove it. Or are you…" Dominic's voice drifted away and looking down he saw that Famine had hold of one of his wrists, his strong, slender fingers making contact with the bare skin under the sleeve.

Dominic's first reaction was to pull away, but he found he couldn't move. He felt cold, and still, and the bright morning sunlight that had moments ago been streaming in through every window of the cab was fading to a pale, listless grey as if the whole world were being washed away. And then he felt it. It was small at first, barely anything at all, a tingle really, deep in the pit of his stomach. But as it grew it became an ache, a heavy, thick throbbing that spread through his guts, turning his insides to ash and dust. His body felt hollow; emptied and weak, and he struggled to hold a single thought in his head. It was hunger. Pure, total, endless hunger that had known neither a bite of food nor a sip of water its entire life, and just as the spirit cried out in agony for the misery to end and for the void to take you, it continued, on and on, and you knew it was your fate to know nothing other than this feeling for all of time.

"Hotel Alexander, safe and sound," came the cab driver's cheerful voice.

Dominic blinked, his eyes feeling dry and gritty, and he stared about himself in a panic. Outside the cab windows, the street bustled with people going about their day; the traffic flowing smoothly through the heart of the city, and a hundred and one different sounds echoed off the tall buildings on either side of them. A wide, gold-trimmed glass doorway, the name 'Alexander' etched across the middle, stood waiting to Dominic's left, and the cab driver was sat patiently in the driver's seat.

"How did we…?" Dominic stuttered.

"I did try to warn you, Dom," the cab driver smiled. "First visit to the city, it can be a lot to take in."

"You showed me," Dominic muttered.

"Yes, I suppose I did," the cab driver replied softly.

When Dominic had pulled himself together enough, he paid the fare and exited the cab, dragging his large suitcase out after him. He stared up at the front of the hotel building for a moment, then turned back to the cab, leaning down to speak through the open front window.

"Will I see you again?" he asked.

The cab driver turned, smiling. "You may do. It's a big city, and there are an awful lot of cabs about. But yes, you never know, do you?"

With that the cab pulled away from the curb and joined the flow of traffic, eventually disappearing from sight, although Dominic stayed put for a while, watching the long line of cars coming and going. A faint grumble in his stomach reminded him that he hadn't yet eaten, and turning away from the road, Dominic began to climb the steps up to the hotel, thinking that he would like to find somewhere close by for a little lunch.

AUTHOR BIO — DALE PARNELL

Dale Parnell lives in Staffordshire, with his wife and their imaginary dog, Moriarty. He writes short fiction, mainly fantasy, science-fiction, and horror, along with the occasional poem. He has self-published three books to date and is lucky enough to feature in a number of fiction and poetry anthologies.

THE ESCAPE
by Leanne Cooper

"Airport, please." She says, glancing up and catching the wrinkled, hazel eyes of the cab driver reflected in the rear-view mirror.

"Off anywhere nice?" he asks.

She catches a lingering twang in the thick cockney voice, that has her wondering where the accent originated. Certain that she had heard it somewhere before, she tries to think back to where, or from whom; but unable to place it, she quickly gives up, figuring that it was a nice lilt, and she should just enjoy the change to the typical gruff voices of the cab drivers she had had before.

"I hope so," she sighed apprehensively. Truth be told, Lydia had no definitive plan. She had packed a suitcase, and a few necessities - including her faded passport (still in date ... just about), and the wad of cash she had secretly been saving for the past few months - into an oversized handbag a couple of weeks ago. They had been hidden in the utility cupboard, waiting for the perfect opportunity for her to grab them and get out. Lydia had been worried that her luggage would be discovered but reminded herself that Leroy never bothered himself with household chores, let alone knew how to even switch on a washing machine, so there would not be any need for him to be in the utility cupboard. There was always that small chance though, which sent her anxiety into overdrive every time she thought about it, but it turned out she was correct in her assumption, so her plan came together nicely - thank God!

Now, sat in the back of a trundling black cab, she could breathe a sigh of relief. She had done it. She had escaped the house and all that it represented. The hardest part was over now, and she had the world ahead of her; no longer held captive by Leroy's tyranny, and need to be in control. She was free to go where she wanted, do what she wanted, and be who she wanted to be.

Suddenly, the buzzing of a phone pulls her away from her thoughts.

"Sorry, love, mind if I take this call on the headset? I wouldn't usually, but it's important."

The driver was apologetic, and she could tell by his pleading eyes in the mirror that this was essential. A family matter, perhaps? She hoped it wasn't anything serious or upsetting and nodded as she told him it was no problem. Traffic was at a standstill as per usual, so she didn't have any issues with him taking the call. She leaned against the cold window, feeling the faintest draft as she wistfully watched people walking by. The driver spoke, but this time in a familiar foreign language. Again, she felt she had heard the voice before, but pushed away the paranoia. London is a huge, multicultural city, filled with people from all over the globe - many of whom speak this language. So, obviously it would be one that she had encountered many times. Switching back to English, the driver ended the call on a pleasant tone. "Yeah, yeah, no worries mucka, I've got it sorted. Ta ra."

He sighs, then glances into the mirror. "Sorry about that, love. All sorted now. And not long until we get you to your destination." "That's no problem... and thank you. It will be a relief when I'm finally on the plane." She chuckles to herself, knowing that the driver will never realise just how much of a relief.

The past couple of years with Leroy had been hell. At first, it had been an amazing whirlwind romance: he had been kind, supportive, and encouraging.

They bought their dream house, had a fancy car, and meals out most nights; but then, as the money dwindled, he changed. He was no longer happy - always wanting more, expecting more from her; and what started out as gentle persuasion, now become more forceful... more pressure for her to do what he wanted. She didn't want that, told him she was happy, loved him regardless of how much money he had. That just made his temper worse, he was insistent that she do what he told her to. In his head she owed him, and he hated how ungrateful she was being. Well, now she had built up the courage to leave, she was going to show him

34

that she didn't need him. She could go this alone.

Finally, the cab pulls up outside the airport. Parking in the drop-off point, the driver gets out of the vehicle and opens the door. "I'm sorry that the journey took longer than expected. Typical though, ain't it?" He hauls the suitcase out and places it onto the walkway. It's one of those new types, the expensive ones that have four wheels on the bottom that glide easily as they are pulled along, not one of those awkward style cases that have to be tilted and end up flopping from side to side due to the flimsiness of the pull-out handle.

Taking Lydia's hand, he helps her step out of the taxi. "You gonna be ok with this and your bag?" He asks, nodding towards the leather handbag she is clutching protectively. Looking down, she notices an exquisite ruby ring, set in Asian gold on his left ring finger, and notes that it is oddly extravagant for someone on taxi driver wages.
"I'll be fine, thank you." She tells him, handing him a few 20's, "keep the change."
"Tar, love. Have a good flight," he says whilst sliding into the driver's seat.

She waits on the pavement long enough to watch him drive through the barrier, then heads past the bustling crowd of people, to the looming automatic doors. "Almost there." She braces herself, and steps through as the doors slide apart, allowing her to continue forward.

Lydia stands in front of the outbound flight board; names of countries illuminated above her head, glowing invitingly. The only question on her mind now is where exactly should she go? Deciding it best to check which flights have available seats, and choosing between those, she heads to the ticket desk; working her way past important-looking men in suits with briefcases instead of suitcases, reunited - or departing- lovers in a tight embrace, kissing each other passionately, and frenzied families hurrying by - small children, dragged along by hands or elbows as they fail to keep up the pace. There is quite a queue at the desk. Impatient men and women tutting, sighing, or even muttering to themselves, annoyed at having to wait. Lydia could understand that though. She too was impatient to get going, but unlike them, she wasn't in a race against time to get to the boarding gate before the last call was given.

As she stood there, daydreaming of warm beaches, and cold Pina Coladas, she could feel a pain in her arm. Long fingers squeezing the flesh just above the crook of her elbow, and hot breath scorching her ear. Her heart racing, eyes darting in panic, as the instantly recognisable voice, smooth like whisky, whispers: "Don't make a sound, my darling, I've got you now, come with me." There is nowhere to run. No choice but to follow Leroy. He casually puts his bronzed arm around her shoulders, letting it drape softly enough that a stranger would get the impression of a caring husband, but grasping her arm tight enough to remind her that he has all of the power. His thick black hairs tickle against her neck and bare shoulders. She never really liked hairy men, but it only served to make Leroy more masculine. She remembered how lying on his broad, fur-covered chest once made her feel safe and protected. Now, that which made him more manly only reminded her of how weak she was against him. "I'm sorry... I'm sorry, ok? Just let go of me," she hisses as she's led forcefully back out of the building. Leroy softly shushes her. If not for the situation at hand, it would have done a good job of soothing her. "Now, now, Princess." His lips press against the top of her head. She cringes at the no-longer welcome affection.

Once outside, Leroy stops at the edge of the pathway and hails a waiting black cab that shuttles forward a few feet to line up with them. Leroy raps with his knuckle onto the closed passenger side window. As it rolls down, Lydia becomes overwhelmed with dread and confusion.
"Hello, again, love. Miss your flight did ya?" It's her cab driver. But how? Sniggering he winks knowingly up at Leroy, who has become the epitome of smugness.
"Oh, my Angel, did you not recognise Ali without his balaclava?" He feigns a sympathetic look, before snatching her handbag, throwing it into the cab, and pinning her to the wall. His face contorted with anger, he grabs Lydia's chin between his thumb

and forefinger, forcing her to look at him. She clenches her eyes shut, refusing to look him in the eye. Shit. She really fucked up big time. She should have known not to go up against Leroy.

"I loved you. You were the only woman I ever loved. I would have given you the world, and all the riches you could ever dream of. Why do this to me? Why break my heart, huh?" He lets go of Lydia's chin, softly strokes her face, and plants a kiss on her forehead. She can smell the deep musk of Hugo Boss. A part of her wants to nuzzle into his neck and savour it, but all she can say is, "I'm sorry Leroy. I wanted out and you couldn't accept that. I needed to make a new life for myself, away from the crime, away from your mob of miscreant friends. When you forced me to do that one last heist, I thought I could use it to my advantage. Take the money and run."
"Oh, Angel," he chuckles, shaking his head at her the way a parent might at finding amusement in something mischievous a toddler has done; but then he stares into her eyes, his voice serious, and maybe, could it be...? A bit sad? "I will forgive you of anything, my love. You are my weakness, after all. I would never want to harm you." He looks back at Ali counting notes from the wad of cash hidden in the handbag, then turns back to face her, Lydia's eyes now wide with fear staring back at him. "But the boys...? Well... they're not so forgiving. You have really upset them, after all. And what a silly girl, thinking you could get through customs with all that money. You should have stolen my car as well as my money, No?" Turning to the cab, he asks, "Ali, have you taken your cut now?"
"Oh yes, mucka, I'm all sorted and ready to go, when you are, boss."

Although Leroy had already loosened his grip, Lydia remained frozen in place. Too scared to move, her brain racing with anticipation of what might come next. How foolish she was to take the entire loot. Too greedy. She should have waited until the prearranged time that the money was shared out, given the lads their share, and bolted. Too late for regrets and what-ifs. It all made sense now though - those wrinkled hazel eyes, the accent, and that expensive ring. The ring that SHE had grabbed from the display cabinet of the jewellers during that job back in March. "Thanks, Darling," the balaclava covered giant had said as she had handed it over to him. It dawned on her that her clever plan was not as clever as she had thought. Leroy must have figured it out long ago and plotted his revenge.

"I have to go now, my love. Good luck, you will need it."

With that the cab drives off, Leroy kisses her one last time on the lips, then climbs into a jet black 1962 Chevrolet Corvette, cruising off behind the cab. "Ciao, Bella." He blows a kiss, and waves as he speeds away, leaving her standing alone watching the barrier close behind him, scared of what will become of her.

AUTHOR BIO – LEANNE COOPER

Leanne Cooper is a Poet, and Author from the West Midlands, who since her debut in 2017, has gone on to perform across the Midlands and Stafford, including the Wolverhampton Literary Festival as part of Poets Against Racism.
Leanne has been published both online, and in print for various anthologies, and has released 2 of her own poetry collections - 'Awake at 3 AM', and 'All For You' - both of which can be found on Amazon.

THE CONFESSIONAL
BY DAVID BOWMORE

The door closed with a clunk. The cabbie, eyes on the passenger, waited as the old man buckled himself into the backseat.

"Where to?"

"Not sure really, anywhere," the passenger replied with a hacking phlegm-filled cough.

"Right-o." The cabbie didn't mind. Some fares were like that, needing a bit of peace or solitude or time to think. So, the black cab pulled out and joined the constant flow of traffic sloshing through the wet capital; meter ticking over, and doors automatically locking.

"Everything alright back there?"

The old man had discreetly hawked into a handkerchief.

"Oh fine, fine. You don't mind driving around for a few minutes, do you?"

"It's your money, grandad."

The old man chuckled. Cabbies were always good value.

"I suppose you've had a few faces in here, haven't you?" It was the normal question to ask.

"You'd be surprised."

"Try me."

"Suppose the most famous was Michael Caine, you know, the actor."

"Really?"

"But that was back in the nineties when I was new to The Knowledge."

"Anyone else?"

"Couple of pop stars that no one remembers. And an actress from one of the soaps was sick in her handbag once."

"Any of these famous people ever tell you any secrets?"

"Now that would be telling," the cabbie said with a wink in the mirror.

The old man took a deep wheezing breath.

The eyes of the cabbie flicked to the rear viewer. The fair didn't look too well.

"It's much like a confessional in here, isn't it?" the old man said. "With this clear panel between us, we can't really see each other properly and our voices are turned into digital ones and zeros. The God of the twenty-first century."

"If you say so," The colourful lights of London by night distorted the cabbie's features.

"Listen to this," the old man said.

* * *

"As you so subtly commented, my school days are way behind me. Nearly sixty years behind me. I still feel young in my heart and up here too. Nothing wrong with my memory. I still remember the good times… and the bad. Pity the body ain't what it used to be, hey? This bloody emphysema will be the death of me. Too many cigarettes they say.

I had my first smoke with Martin Coombs behind the bike shed at school. I was twelve. In those days, you left school when you were fifteen unless you wanted to go to the polytechnic. We called it "the tech". I didn't go to the tech.

Martin was my best friend. We sat together in every class. Me and Martin had been friends since we could walk and went everywhere together. When we were younger, we would scrump for apples at the risk of being caught by the farmer, or we'd tramp for miles along the riverbank, skimming stones and looking for bits of downed Messerschmitts, talking about the future and what we'd do when we were grown-up. We didn't know life was hard. When we became older the need for money forced us into summer jobs. Martin worked on a stall in the meat market three days a week and I got a job collecting glasses and washing up in one of the market pubs – The Dog and Duck. Both eye-opening experiences for fourteen-year-old boys. We would exchange horrific tales of our respective workplaces. Bloody fights in the pub from me. Filthy hygiene practice from Martin. But the money seemed like a fortune to us and with it came an ability to impress the girls.

I was soon able to buy my own clothes and didn't need to rely on my older brother's hand-me-downs. A rockabilly haircut and a pair of winkle-pickers soon had the girls looking at us when we went back to school after the summer holiday.

Me and Martin teamed up with a pair of lookers from the girls' school on the other side of the road, St. Catherine's. Jean was blonde and Noreen wasn't but that didn't matter. We weren't really interested in the colour of their hair. We'd all go to the cinema and not watch the film in the back row. As young men, we felt fortunate to cop a feel and were soon rebuked if we went too far. Although Noreen was more adventurous than Jean. At least that's what Martin led me to believe.

And then he told me he'd done the dirty deed with Jean a couple of nights earlier, while I'd been at work. And then I understood why she said she hadn't wanted to see me anymore. He said he felt bad about it and well, best mates didn't keep secrets from each other, did they?

Of course—and I regret this—I couldn't let it go, could I? I sort of saw red and lashed out. The blow was a good one. I'd learnt a few things from the pub, one of which was how to throw a punch. It caught him on the sweet spot under his chin that snapped his head back. He went down fast and caught the side of his head on the edge of a concrete step. He was very still and there was no blood. I thought he was just, you know, unconscious. But after about ten minutes or so I realised he was most definitely dead.

This happened on the school grounds. It was easy to get into at night and it was a solitary, quiet place. We'd often sit on the steps telling tall tales, smoking, and drinking stout smuggled from my dad's sideboard. We were too old to be hanging around the rec yard and too young to mix with adults in pubs. The school grounds were a discrete place to pretend to be grown up.

It was fortunate for me that a trench was being dug at the bottom of the sports field, so I set to with a shovel and made the hole a little deeper and laid his body in it. Then covered him with some soil. It ruined my clothes, but I got home late enough for no one to notice. I chucked them in one of those old metal rubbish bins outside someone's house a few streets away on my way to school the next morning. It was collection day.

From my place next to a window in maths class, I saw the workmen lowering big clay pipes on top of Martin.

A few days later the police wanted to know when I'd last seen him. And they believed me when I said I hadn't seen him since school on Wednesday and that he'd never met up with me when he should have. His body has never been discovered. My friend was simply written off as a runaway. His poor mother never understood why he'd gone and pestered me for months. She thought I must have known something.

But how could I ease her suffering?

I was suffering, too.

I missed my best friend, still do for that matter. We'd have got over the girl. I hadn't meant to kill him.

But I absolutely knew what I was doing when I slit Jean's throat a year later, although I take no responsibility. After all, Martin's death was all her fault.

And after that, I sort of got a taste for it. Murder. Only ever women and always from different backgrounds. Never two in a row in the same county. Never the same way of offing them twice; rope, candlestick, gun. I'm very good at Cluedo.

And sometimes, years passed before I felt the urge again. I'm not a pervert or anything sick like that. I just like killing women. I'm good at it. I just put an old dear called Norma out of her misery with a pillow. A quick death is good for everyone involved."

* * *

"Pull the other one, grandad," the cabbie said, passing the Houses of Parliament onto Westminster Bridge. No one would ever come out with a story like that if it were true. And the old bloke certainly didn't look senile. A sick mind perhaps – but he was no killer.

"I knew you wouldn't believe me." The old man coughed again. This time, the fit lasted for several minutes, bending him over. Clearly, the story had exhausted him.

"So, where do you want to go?" The cabbie asked with a worried glance in the mirror.

Silence from the back of the cab.

"Oi, mister. You alright?"

"Better... take me... to... hospital." His breath came in short gasps.

"Oh, shit!"

At the E.R entrance of the nearest hospital, St. Thomas', the cab came to an ungainly stop and, leaving the engine running, the driver dashed inside for help, returning with two orderlies only to find the old man toppled forward, his seatbelt straining to keep him upright, blood running down his chin and the front of his coat, onto the floor of the cab.

A piece of paper fell from the old man's hand as they struggled to get him out of the cab and onto a trolley. Words were being thrown around that the cabbie only half-understood; cardiac, intravenous, blood pressure.

The cabbie picked the folded piece of paper up and slid it into a trouser pocket, intending to follow them inside.

"Do you know his name?" someone asked.

44

"No. I'm just the cabbie."

"No need to come inside," someone said.

The cabbie drove home, 'for hire' light off. It wouldn't be possible to take another fare till the mess and blood had been cleared up and that couldn't be done in the dark, not properly.

In the driveway, listening to the engine tick and tock as it cooled, and thinking about the unlikely story the passenger had told, the cabbie wondered what the best course of action would be. No one could do what the old man had claimed to have done and never be caught, could they? Perhaps the police should be told? But the old boy was probably dead by now—would it make any difference? He hadn't looked too chipper as they wheeled him away.

"Shit, the piece of paper." The cabbie had meant to give it back, but with all the commotion and the quick brush off from the staff, had completely forgotten.

Unfolding the A4 paper, realization dawned. The handwriting was neat, sloping and fresh, and recently written with a quality pen and ink.

Both sides had three columns, headed; name, dates, and means of murder. The oldest. **Martin Coombs - September 1958 - Accident.**

The list continued…

Until under Norma's row, and with today's date, was her own name.

Louise Lake; means of death – Poison Pen.

AUTHOR BIO — DAVID BOWMORE

David Bowmore lives in Yorkshire with his wonderful wife and a small white poodle.

He has worn many hats in his time; chef, teacher, and landscape gardener.

Since 2018, David's stories have been published in more than fifty anthologies.

His award-winning book of connected short stories, The Magic of Deben Market, and his best of collection, Tall Tales & Short Fiction, are available in paperback and Kindle through Amazon.

More information can be found on his website
www.davidbowmore.co.uk

THE BLACK CAB
BY NICOLE

A middle-class looking man in a rigid business suit stepped out of a black London cab on a Thursday afternoon into the drizzling grey.

It wasn't a modern or ordinary-looking black cab, but older, probably from the '60s or '70s, and very worn looking. It had definitely seen better days.

The stern-faced man hadn't even considered this when he had gotten into the cab fifteen minutes earlier. He was running late and had hailed the first cab he had seen.

He stepped out of the car in front of his Camden town flat and walked calmly up the steps to his front door. His face was emotionless, and his urgency was gone. He strode past his wife who greeted him with the usual. "Hi love, how was your day," like she did every day. Her words were ignored, however, and he continued up the stairs.

Perplexed, she called after him again and then followed. She found him upstairs holding his hunting rifle. Before she could register what was happening, he had shot her two times in the chest, and then put the gun in his mouth.

The middle-aged burly detective stood over two dead bodies in a posh Camden town flat. Blood soaked a floral rug of which the original calming shades of beige were now a dark murky red. "I just don't understand the sense in this," he muttered, "there just doesn't seem to be any motivation."

Another detective, this one much younger, shook his head in agreement. "I know boss, he had no financial issues, there are no fishy transactions in his accounts, and according to his colleagues, the guy was doing great at work. I talked with friends and family as well, and they all say their marriage was fine too."

The older detective looked up at him and gestured towards him. "See if you can track his movements through the day and let's see if anything happened. I know this is an open and shut murder-suicide, but this one has me a little curious."

The young detective nodded as he said, "right-o boss, I'll get on it." As he scuttled off to fulfill his duties, the remaining detective took a glance back down at the gruesome scene, shook his head, and walked out.

A sixteen-year-old girl stood waiting outside a prep school impatiently tapping her foot. It was Thursday, and she had dance practise soon. How could her mother forget? She always forgot because she was always working. She pulled out her mobile and pressed her mother's name to dial the number.

"Straight to voicemail…typical," she muttered before jamming the phone back into her bag. She looked down the street, hoping to see her mother's car. Nothing appeared. She was about to yell out an expletive when her bag began to vibrate. She quickly picked up the phone and heard her mother's familiar voice.

"Where the hell are you mother?" she screamed into the phone.

Her mother responded with a nonchalant tone, "Darling I've been stuck at an exhibition and am running late, can you take a taxi home please and I will meet you there to take you to dance practise."

The girl shouted, "FINE," and threw the phone on the ground. As she bent down to pick it up, an old black cab creaked up to the kerb and stopped in front of her. The girl was startled but soon shouted directions at the anonymous man in front and got in. The dark-haired man in the front said nothing and started driving. When he pulled up outside of her terraced house in Camden Town, she stepped out of the cab and stood on the pavement. Her face was stoic, and she walked almost in slow motion to the front door. Upon hearing the door open, her mother shouted. "Oh good, you're back, if you get changed quickly, we might just make it on time." The catatonic girl stepped into the kitchen where her mother's back was turned, picked up the knife, being used to chop celery into sticks, off of the chopping block, and stabbed her mother in the back five times, and then stabbed herself in the chest.

"Hey Boss," the young detective said as he saw his superior enter the room. "I checked up on that guy, and it turns out he had a pretty normal day. He finished at the office and said goodbye to some clients, got in a cab, and went home. Maybe he just snapped."

"Thanks for doing that," the burly one replied. "Go ahead and write up the report and file it if you don't mind; meanwhile I'm heading out to check out our second murder-suicide of the day."

"Another one?" the young detective replied with surprise.

"Yeah, a mother and daughter," he murmured, "guess I'm not getting away with the missus this weekend. Honestly, this shit is getting old."

"Hey, Hun, would you mind closing up shop today for me? I have a hot date tonight." The forty-something-year-old woman smiled cheekily at her employee.

"Yeah, yeah, yeah, go on, get your groove on," said a relenting young man, probably in his early twenties, as he waved at her and chuckled to himself.

"Oh, you're a gem, thanks so much babe," she said as she whisked herself off and out the door. The young man watched as she flailed her arms to hail a cab, and then, once successful, jumped into a vintage-looking black cab.

"Huh," he muttered to himself, "surprised that piece of junk is still running." Then he sighed and started counting money from the till.

The burly detective struggled to duck under some blue and white police tape which had been awkwardly placed at a level where he could not easily step over or under it. After effing and blinding about incompetent underlings for a few seconds, he approached the local officer who had clearly been left to guard the door to the crime scene. He assumed this guy had been the schmuck who had placed the police tape so awkwardly, and briefly thought of having a go at him, and then thought better of it. Instead, he said, "Jesus H Christ, what do we have now? I'm never going to get a goddamn holiday."

The startled underling jumped and stuttered, "Oo, oh, sorry ssss…sir. I don't really know anything so far, just that a local shop owner murdered who we think is her boyfriend, and then killed herself."

The burly one stared in disbelief at the almost trembling officer. 'What the hell is going on,' he thought briefly and then let himself in the front door.

Upon first looking at the scene, he had to turn away from the gruesome sight. He had been working dead bodies for 20 years and had never had to look away. Was he going soft? "What in the hell happened here?" he said to the young detective who was kneeling on the floor placing a sample of something, with some tweezers, into a labeled plastic bag. The young detective looked up. "From what I can see, this unfortunate man's girlfriend knocked him out with a blunt instrument, possibly this saucepan, and then strapped his face down on the hob with duct tape and let him burn to death."

"My God, are we sure that it was her? Maybe it was a home invasion?"

The young detective shook his head, "there are no other fingerprints present, no forced entry, nothing stolen, and her fingerprints are all over the saucepan, hob, and the duct tape." He continued, "of course, I'm going to look into this one a bit more as it isn't as cut and dry as the other murder-suicides we have seen this week. I'll run some tests to double-check the saucepan is our primary blunt weapon, but it seems like it is."

The burly detective made a puzzled face and then spoke, "well what happened to her?" The young detective pointed towards the garage. "She gave herself a much more peaceful death."

There she was, slumped over the driver's seat, with her lips blue and her face swollen. It was the classic peaceful suicide method of killing yourself with the fumes from your car. "Well, she got off easy," he muttered with a disgusted look on his face, "unlike the poor bastard in the kitchen."

He returned to the young detective. "So, do we have a motive at all?" The young detective shook his head, "not really. I suppose it's possible he tried to assault her, and she fought back, but she has no defensive wounds whatsoever. Not to mention this is pretty extreme retaliation."

The burly detective interrupted, "Do we know of her movements at all? Have you spoken to friends and family?"

The young detective shook his head again, "She has no family nearby, and all I got from her shop assistant was that she left a little before closing, hopped in an old black cab and that was the last he saw of her."

The burly detective started pacing as he spoke, "I just feel like this is insane. Three murder-suicides all in one day, all in Camden Town. I feel like this has to be connected in some way, but I just don't get it."

The young detective spoke up cautiously, "I don't see how they can be connected. As far as I am aware, none of these people knew each other. Of course, I can do some more digging if you want, but I imagine the chief is going to want this wrapped up pretty quickly."

The burly one started to walk away, but turned back to the other detective, "keep digging please, but keep it quiet. I know there has to be some connection here, but I have no idea what it is. I've got to find it. I've had enough for today, I'm heading home to try and make amends with the wife for being so late, and most likely cancelling our holiday this weekend." He tossed the keys for the patrol car towards the young detective. "You take the car back tonight; I'll just catch a cab. I need to think, and I can't focus on driving in this shit traffic right now."

The young detective nodded. "Right-O boss, see ya tomorrow."

The burly detective walked outside into the heavy drizzle. He lit up a cigarette, took a drag, and started walking towards the main road. He was dreading arriving home late. She was getting fed up and was probably going to leave him soon. He'd come home one day and find her gone, and it would be his fault.

'Whatever,' he thought. 'All good things must come to an end eh?' He leaned forward and stubbed out his cigarette on a nearby tree. He looked up as an old black cab pulled up in front of him and stopped.

'Christ, that's an ancient piece of shit,' he thought to himself.

He flicked his cigarette butt into the air and got into the cab.

AUTHOR BIO — NICOLE

Nicole is a multi-talented artist. She plays numerous instruments; she can sing and now she writes as well. Nicole loves bike riding and has competed on many levels. She enjoys a glass of Cava and good tapas, whilst snuggled up with her hubby, son, and their dog called Brodie.

A PINKY PROMISE
BY FRASER SMITH

The black cab pulled up at the side of the road. The driver turned around and stared at the woman asleep on the cold black leather back seat.

"Hey Luv, Rothwell avenue," he said gruffly.

The woman stirred but didn't wake; she was young, around 24 or 25. She was wearing a black and white chequered dress. The driver couldn't help but take another look at the long thin legs stretched out diagonally across the back of his vehicle. He opened the driver's door and walked round to the curb. He was a short man with a large beer belly; he opened the passenger door of his taxi and shook the woman gently.

"Hey, sleepy Jean, 41 Rothwell avenue"

She awoke with a jump.

"Ohhh," she murmured. "How much do I owe you?"

"Euston to Streatham, £34.20 doll, the wake-up call was free." He chuckled to himself as he got back into the driver's seat.

She rummaged in her handbag for her purse, locating it, she undid the clasp and produced two rolled up £20 notes. She prodded them under the Perspex screen that divided her from the driver. The driver was already searching through his red cloth bag of change when she told him not to bother.

"You sure doll?" he asked, surprised. "That's very kind of you."

She clambered out of the open door, reaching back in to pick up her case, which had spent the journey next to her on the back seat. She slammed the door shut and the taxi slowly moved away. Looking up at the black front door, she lifted her case and slowly walked up the steps. She rang the doorbell.

"Ni-Ni! You made it." Hannah Davies squealed with delight when she saw her best friend standing on her doorstep.

"Come in, come in," she said.

Nilima Suglani dropped her case in the hallway, and the two friends embraced.

"It's so good to see you."

Hannah led Nilima into the lounge. The room was large, stretching from the front to the back of the house. Two thread-bare coffee-coloured sofas faced each other in the front part of the room. The two sofas were separated by a long pine glassed topped coffee table. A flat-screen television hung on the chimney breast on the right-hand wall. The back of the room was given over to a small round wooden kitchen table and a large imposing bookcase.

"Take a seat," Hannah gestured to Nilima to sit down. Nilima sank into one of the sofas.

"Are you sure it's ok for me to stay?" she asked her friend.

"Don't be silly, of course, it is," Hannah laughed. "Tony is out of town this weekend, visiting his folks in Leeds, you can have his bed, he won't mind, it'll be the first time a woman has actually slept in it." She gave Nilima a knowing wink.

"Is the jury still out then?" Nilima asked.

"Oh yes," Hannah said, "No signs either way."

As soon as the words left her lips there was a thunder of footsteps on the stairs and Mark, Hannah's younger brother, came bursting into the room.

"Hi Ni," Mark exclaimed moving over to the sofa, "I thought I heard the door."

Nilima stood up and they pecked each other on the cheek.

"Do you want to come for a drink? We're heading down The Alex if you fancy it, just for an hour or so," Mark enquired.

"Not tonight, thanks," Nilima said. "I'm so tired, I was on the ward at 6 this morning. Han, is it ok if I grab a shower?"

"Of course, the bathroom is upstairs, first door on the left, Tony's room is the one next door to that. Have you eaten? Shall we have a takeaway?"

"Sure," Nilima said.

"Chinese?" Hannah asked.

"Sounds good." She smiled weakly, "there's money in my purse."

"Nonsense, tonight it's on me." Hannah beamed.

Nilima gave another weak smile and made her way upstairs with her case.

After her shower Nilima put on her pyjamas and made her way back to the lounge. Her dark hair, still damp, fell in curls down her back. When she reached the lounge the coffee table was filled with food.

"Come on tuck in," Hannah demanded, "I didn't know what you wanted so there's Chow Mein, rice, duck, chicken and...," she held up a small plastic container, prodding the contents with a fork, "I think this is shrimp."

The two women sat down and ate, Hannah had opened a bottle of wine and poured two glasses.

After they had eaten, Hannah turned to her friend and said: "Do you remember when we were kids, standing on that hill looking out over the city, we made the pinky promise we would always be there and never judge each other no matter what we did?"

Nilima laughed "I sure do."

As the two old friends looked at each other and laughed, the front door opened, and Mark appeared in the lounge with a tall, thin man in a black leather jacket.

"Ni, this is Davie, he's a good friend of mine," Mark said.

Nilima stood up from the sofa and offered her hand to Davie.

"Lovely to meet you," she said.

"Likewise," Davie said, he had a rich Glaswegian accent. "Mark's been telling me all about you, lovely to finally put a face to the name."

56

"Only good things I hope," Nilima giggled.

"Of course," Davie replied.

"I'm going to be terribly rude and call it a night," Nilima said, making her way over to the hall.

"I hope not on my account?" Davie replied.

"Not at all," Nilima countered, "It's just been a long day, g' night."

As her footsteps on the stairs faded away and they heard the click of an upstairs door shut, Hannah, Mark, and Davie made themselves comfortable on the sofas. Hannah stretched out in the space where a few moments before Nilima had been, while the two men made do with sharing the sofa opposite.

"So, that's the famous Nilima?" Davie said with a grin, "I didn't expect her to be so beautiful."

"Seriously Davie," Hannah looked disgusted.

Davie threw back his head and laughed, "I'm only playing," he said, "tell me about what happened, as you were there, obviously I know what I saw on the news at the time, but you guys were first-hand witnesses."

"Not quite," Hannah responded.

"Come on, don't be coy," Davie said.

Mark looked at his sister, "It's probably better coming from us, you know that if anyone recognises Ni in the next few days tongues are going to wag, so we might as well tell Davie the truth."

Hannah thought for a moment and reluctantly agreed.

"You know I don't like talking about this, but you're right, but I'm telling Davie, you were too young to remember most of it anyway."

Hannah poured herself another glass of wine before continuing.

"Well, you know we say our parents are quite conservative?"

Davie nodded.

"Well, that's how we meet Ni, Ni's parents were local councillors the same as our parents, you know they'd have all these dinner parties where they'd put the world to rights and they would circle jerk over Thatcher, that kind of thing. Well, Ni's mother was like an Indian version of Thatcher. There were rumours she was going to stand for Mayor of the borough and she'd probably have won it as well, she was an amazing speaker, could hold a room for hours."

"What about Ni's dad?" Davie enquired.

"Ni's father used to own grocery shops."

"The typical Indian newsagents." laughed Davie.

"Oh, much bigger than that, these places did everything and they were goldmines he became quite well off. He decided to invest in property, he bought a few houses; did them up, a lick of paint here and there, and then rented them out. Ni's mum took care of these properties while her dad concentrated on his businesses, she would interview the tenants, do inspections, and arrange any work that needed doing."

Davie looked amazed.

"Sounds like they had quite a little empire going."

"They did, the profits from the business were put aside for Ni. Mrs Suglani took the profits from the houses and paid for the household expenses. One of the houses was rented to a couple, you know seemed a nice sort, they had three children, one day out of the blue the wife leaves the husband, took the kids, the lot. Mrs Suglani took pity on this chap she would pop round and do the cleaning for him, cook him meals, that kind of thing. I remember the day it happened like it was yesterday."

"The fire?" Davie asked, leaning forward on the edge of his seat.

"Yep," continued Hannah, "when the firefighters eventually got inside the house, guess what they saw? Mrs Suglani and this guy naked in one of the bedrooms. It seemed like Mrs Prim and Proper was having a bit on the side and it turns out it had been going on for a year or more. The wife had found out you see, so she had upped and left with the kids. So, when the firefighters found the bodies, they carried out the investigation and everything pointed to arson. The first person they looked to was this guy's wife, but she had a cast-iron alibi; she was 150 miles away at her mother's house in Nottingham. All eyes then turned to Mr Suglani and he was arrested. As we were so close to the family and me and Ni were best friends, Ni came to live with us. What else could my parents do? It was either that or Ni going into care."

"And her father got sent down for life?" Davie asked, seeking confirmation.

"Yeah," It was Mark's turn now to continue the story, "He got two life sentences, he always protested his innocence, but the evidence was overwhelming, he had a few lock-up garages that he used to store stock. When the police searched them, in one they found a half-filled jerry can of petrol, inside were rags the same type that the fire service had said were used to start the fire."

"So, where was Nilima, when her dad was torching this house?" Davie enquired.

"Upstairs in her bedroom doing her homework, she was always a clever kid who loved school, so he knew she would be up there for hours. He must've slipped out and done the deed while she worked. You see, the house was only a few streets away from the family home, and the lock-up was on the way. He could have been there and back within half an hour. During the trial Nilima gave evidence via video, they asked her if her father left the house that afternoon, she said 'not to her knowledge but she was upstairs until the police knocked at the front door', get this: they woke him up as well, he was fast asleep on the sofa, you know the kind of thing you do, after burning your wife and her lover to death."

"Wow!" Davie appeared to be in shock at everything he was hearing. "And then he topped himself?"

"Yeah, he hanged himself, about six months after going inside. There was a big enquiry because he was meant to be on suicide watch."

"That poor wee girl," Davie looked like he had tears in his eyes.

"Ni-Ni is a brilliant woman, she doesn't want pity, she never has," Hannah said. "After everything she's been through, she still went to university and is now a doctor in Manchester, she's done well for herself." Hannah got up from where she had been sitting, stretched, and yawned. She looked at her watch, "God it's late, I'm going up to bed."

The following day dawned bright; Sunlight shone in through the window onto Nilima's face. She opened her eyes and laid silent and still for a moment, taking in the unfamiliar surroundings. She rose and made her way to the bathroom. When she made it downstairs Hannah was already up, the television was broadcasting a cookery program and two empty mugs had replaced the wine glasses from the night before on the coffee table. Breakfast consisted of coffee, scrambled eggs, bacon, and anything else Hannah could find to cook. After they had eaten, they both collapsed onto the sofas.

Nilima smiled at her friend and probed gently, "Mark's friend Davie, how long have you known him?"

"Couple of years, why? Urghh, you're not thinking of you know?" Hannah made a circle with the fingers of one hand and inserted the index finger of her other hand into the hole.

They both giggled.

"Maybe, would you be ok with that?" Nilima asked.

"It doesn't bother me. I shouldn't think it'll bother Mark either, I mean at least Tony's bed would see some action at last." Both women giggled again, "We'll go out tonight for dinner, we'll get you dressed up and then come back here, me and Mark will bugger off to bed early."

Nilima smiled, "Sounds like a plan," she said.

A dinner reservation was made at Franco's a local Italian restaurant. Nilima had spent most of the afternoon going through Hannah's wardrobes, trying on various dresses. She had chosen a sleek, short black dress which she matched with sheer black tights and a small black clutch bag. She curled her hair and finally appeared downstairs.

"Woah, you look amazing," Hannah said, staring open-mouthed at her friend. Hannah had chosen a long pale green dress for herself. Mark was already at the restaurant with Davie, so the women made the short walk arm in arm.

The restaurant was a small building located on a street corner. There was a typical mismatch of Italian stereotypes: a large mural of Romeo and Juliet was painted on one wall, the leaning tower of Pisa on the other, the music was just as bad, instrumental versions of 'O sole Mio' and 'Nessun Dorma' seemed to be playing on a continuous loop. The food was good though, large portions of pasta, bread, and wine were devoured. The four friends happily made their way back to the house. As soon as they closed the door Mark and Hannah made their excuses and headed upstairs to their bedrooms.

Nilima and Davie stayed up in the lounge talking. Nilima had found a bottle of wine in the kitchen and two wine glasses were filled.

"I guess you know about my past?" Nilima sprung this question on Davie without warning, he shifted in his seat and looked embarrassed.

"Well…Mark has mentioned…" She stopped him mid-sentence by putting her finger to his lips.

"Shhhhhhh," she said, "Do you want to know a secret?" she whispered.

"Go on then," Davie said.

Before she had a chance to think about what she was saying, she said, "I did it." Then closed her eyes tightly.

"You did what?" questioned Davie, it seemed to him that the room was spinning he wasn't sure if it was the wine or the realisation of what had just been spoken. "You did it," he said quietly, more to himself than to Nilima, "You started the fire?"

A look of fear and shock appeared over Nilima's face, "I've said too much." She tried to get up from the sofa, but the wine had done its job and her legs no longer worked in sync with her brain. She stumbled forwards, and then fell back into the sofa again.

"Talk to me!" Davie said, grabbing both her arms.

"I found them together," she started, "I walked in on them and they were fucking," she buried her face in her hands. "I was 12 Davie. I froze. My mother hit me and called me a nosey whore," Nilima half-smiled. "Ironic, isn't it? I knew then what I had to do. A few weeks later I heard my mother on the phone. She was arranging to meet him at the house. On the day they were meeting, I took the spare key from my mother's drawer. She had several keys to each house, so I knew it wouldn't be missed. After school, I went home as usual and told my father I had loads of homework to do. He would always sit at the table working through the accounts of the shops. My mother was always about here and there doing stuff either in one of the houses or as a councillor, so my father was always home in the afternoons. I made him a cup of tea as usual, but this time I dropped in one of my mother's sleeping tablets. Within an hour he was lying on the sofa, fast asleep. He kept a jerry can in the garage. It was always filled with petrol. He used it for his lawnmower, said he didn't trust electric ones. I put on a pair of gloves which my mother used for gardening and dropped a few cloths in the can. I made my way over to the house. I was frightened someone would see me, but it was October, it was dark, I got lucky no-one did. I let myself into the house and I could hear them upstairs. I pulled the cloths out of the jerry can and laid them in the hallway of the house. There were about five or six cloths and I put them all up the hallway, I splashed petrol up the stairs. I closed the front door as quietly as I could and pulled out a book of matches. I lit a match and dropped it through the letterbox. I will never forget the heat and the light Davie. I ran as fast as I could, my father had a garage which was full of stock I opened that and put the jerry can inside I locked it up, and I went home. My father was still snoring on the sofa." Nilima stopped, she looked over at Davie, his hands covered his face, he was speechless.

"Hannah was the same size as me, she managed to get me a clean school uniform so the police wouldn't smell the petrol."

Davie uncovered his eyes and stared blankly into space.

"Hannah knew?" He asked.

"Of course, Hannah knew," Nilima said, "we made pinky promises, that we'd do anything for each other."

"Including covering up murder?" Davie snapped.

"I think you underestimate the power of two small girl's pinky promises," Nilima responded.

"Why have you told me all this?" Davie cried.

Nilima looked Davie straight in the eye, "I like you, Davie. I've kept this secret for 13 years, I needed to tell someone." She took a deep breath and continued. "I've cried all I could for my parents, I can't cry anymore. I know there is blood on my hands I will never be able to wash off. I studied medicine to save lives because I know I have taken both of my parent's lives. I felt I needed to make amends, but I can't can I? When I'm not at work I sleep because sleeping takes the pain away temporarily at least. Since you first saw me you've been undressing me with your eyes, tonight under the table you couldn't keep your hands off my legs. I loved it, I love the attention, I love how you looked at me with passion, that also took the pain away. I'm going to go upstairs, but I'm telling you, don't follow me. I will ruin your life like I ruined my parents' lives, like I ruined my own life." With that, she gingerly raised herself from the sofa, and holding onto the bannister climbed the stairs. Davie emptied his glass, he walked into the hall, he looked up the stairs stretching out before him, he knew if he climbed them Nilima's body would be stretched out before him too. He put a hand on the door handle of the front door, stopped, and took another look up the stairs.

"It's decision time," he muttered to himself.

The two women walked down the street. The one in a black and white chequered dress pulled a small case, they hailed a cab, it pulled up, stopping a little behind the two women. Nilima opened the door and got in.

"Call me when you're home, Ni."

"I promise," Nilima said, closing the door, she slid the window down. "Pinky promise."

She held out her right pinky and locked onto Hannah's finger like they had all those years before. They both looked at each other, two friends bonded for life. Nilima raised the window.

"Euston Station please." She called to the driver. As the black cab slowly pulled away, she laid back and felt the cold leather on her body. She closed her eyes and slept.

AUTHOR BIO – FRASER SMITH

Fraser Smith is a part-time writer and poet. He is influenced by Stephen King, Franz Kafka, James Joyce, Oscar Wilde, and William Blake. His interests include History, Politics, and football, he is a supporter of Everton and Napoli and lives in East London.

NO 24
BY CHRISTINE KING

Pedro saw the man at the side of the road, his arm out, hailing him. He checked his mirrors and then swung the black cab around to pick up his next fare. The man looked well-dressed but with a rough edge to him, and Pedro wondered briefly if he would be a good tipper.

Debra was sitting by herself at the back of the number 24 bus heading to the town hall, she hated going to a wedding alone, but she couldn't miss her cousin's big day, even if no one had the time to come with her.

On the seat next to her was a brightly wrapped gift, something mundane that the new couple would probably just put in a cupboard and forget about.

Still, she had enjoyed picking it out for the happy couple, the memory of being in that store and looking up from the white porcelain gravy boat, straight into two deep pools of melted chocolate. It was enough to make her blush.

Her hands had shaken, her thighs pulsed, as she stood staring, the handsome owner of those dark, flashing eyes had come over and smiled at her.

They had started to talk, she hardly remembered what she said. She just remembered feeling hot and flustered and that her breasts ached for his touch. She had mostly looked at his lips as they moved, thick and full. Now and then she saw his tongue, and it made her feel dizzy with lust.

They had left the store together, her purchase tucked securely under her arm and him holding her hand.

She placed her hand on top of the present and felt the satin bow, it was soft and smooth, like his skin. Her nether regions tingled as she imagined running her tongue over his tanned chest, his hard erection, and his tightly muscled stomach.

She knew she was going to be late. This bus was crawling through the town, in lines of never-ending traffic, and although she should be thinking of other things she was lost in thoughts of happier times. Yesterday, in fact. Lying in bed with Pedro. Lovely, energetic Pedro who had encouraged her to open her heart, and her legs with his soft Spanish voice and kissable torso.

She was thinking about his hypnotic eyes, lost in a dream, when there he was, driving his black cab. The bus pulled level and she could see him through the window a little ahead of her, in the driver seat. He was intently watching the lights at the roadworks ahead, waiting for them to turn green. She smiled at the thought of that mouth, that firm, moist mouth and the places it had been. The traffic inched forward, and she glanced around. The bus was empty; it was a sunny day and most people were walking along and enjoying the unseasonable warmth, seeing she was alone, no passengers on board, and the driver in his little booth closed off at the front, it made her feel brave.

She willed the bus to pull up a little more, to get closer to the front, her gaze was fixed on her prize and she had a naughty thought.

If the bus moved closer, if she caught his eye, she would do something, something to get his motor racing, and to show him she was ready for another round, ready to tangle herself in his arms and wrap her legs around him. She was sure he had enjoyed their sessions as much as she had, and she was sure he would be up for another one as soon as she reminded him of what was on offer.

Her wish was granted the bus drove slowly ahead and he looked straight at her. His eyes widened in surprise, but he was very happy to see her, his mouth smiled, and his frown disappeared. He gave a little wave with one hand, lifting it from the wheel and wiggling his long, talented fingers.

Debra kissed the window passionately and left a smeared lipstick mark across the glass, then before she could chicken out, she lifted her top and pressed her naked chest against the glass. Pedro was smiling wider now, she could see him, he was also looking longingly at her body which was exactly what she had hoped to achieve. He blew her a kiss and licked his lips.

A car honked, and Pedro looked at the road ahead, pressing the accelerator to follow the line of traffic. The cab moved and there in the back was the passenger, looking out of the side window, his expression horrified and disgusted.

Debra looked into the face of her shocked husband and knew he had seen everything. She pulled her body away from the glass, red-faced and caught, then watched Luther's angry glare race away in the back seat of her lover's cab.

Pedro was smiling to himself. That woman was a crazy one, but eager.

He thought about calling her but would have to wait to drop off his fare. He was going to some business meeting, it was all the man in the back had been ranting about, annoyed he was missing a wedding. He was glad his fare was being quiet now. Pedro glanced in the rear-view mirror in case the man had fallen asleep, but he seemed awake, his jacket was off, and he was seething silently, staring out of the window, at one point he looked at Pedro's licence and Pedro worried that he was going to complain about him or his driving, but then he sat back again and just looked generally annoyed. Pedro couldn't wait to drop him off, the man wafted an air of menace and looked a little unstable.

The customer barked instructions and Pedro followed them, sure the man was wrong, this was the bad end of town. Usually, he didn't pick up from around here, drug dealers and prostitutes stalked the street at night, even now on a sunny day, its dilapidated buildings looked grey and uninviting.

He turned into the side street his passenger indicated and stopped by a run-down old house. It looked deserted, but if this was where his fare was heading, who was he to argue?

He opened the partition, turning to speak to the man in the back. A bunched-up fist came through it, hitting him squarely on the nose and he fell against the dash-board, his hands came up and grabbed his face, his nose was bleeding, the blood ran down into his mouth, it was hot and tasted like metal.

Pedro was aware that the door in the rear of the cab was opening and then the door next to him opened and someone grabbed his shirt and dragged him onto the dirty road. A boot kicked him as he landed, and he felt his ribs break. He couldn't shout as his mouth was full of blood and his chest felt like it was being sat on by an elephant. He didn't even see the knife held in the large, hairy-knuckled hand, on the end of a long, tattooed arm, until it cut into his neck and silenced his scream.

Debra stood at the entrance to the town hall. She wondered if she should try to call Pedro? Would Luther have left the cab by now? When he came home tonight could she pretend she had been flashing him? Her husband was a brute and insanely jealous but up until now she had managed to keep her affairs secret.

Most of them ended with the guy disappearing or never calling back. Men were so unreliable.

She smiled at a few guests and hardly listened to the young couple repeating their vows.

The moment they walked down the aisle and the music played, she was out of her seat and in the hallway calling Pedro. No answer, she left a quick message and wondered if she dared try Luther's number. As she passed by the gift table on the way out, she could see her gift sat in the centre, piled clumsily on top. Her gift seemed silly now, Pedro had said it was beautiful, a swan gravy boat, but maybe it was not the best thing for newlyweds. She rang him again. Still, no answer. Was he going to be another one of those men who stopped answering her calls? Or dropped out of existence?

As she walked down the steps to hail a taxi to take her to the restaurant for the reception, she saw her husband running up the hill towards her.

She smiled and waved, unsure what else to do.

As Luther arrived, he smiled widely and said, "I cancelled my meeting, after you tracked me down and gave me that little taster, how could I not? Maybe we can sneak off and you can give me the main show?"

Debra was so relieved, she almost cried. "Yes, let's do it."

He might be a dumb brute, but at least her husband was reliable. Unlike Pedro, Danny, Peter, James, and whatever his name had been last month. How many had there been over the years? If her memory served her right this was probably number 24. Was that terrible? Was she an awful wife? She sighed heavily.

Luther held his wife's arm firmly as they climbed into a black cab. He heard her sigh and wondered how long it would take her to get over Pedro? Not long, he guessed, just like all the others. Danny, Peter, James, and whatever his name had been last month.

AUTHOR BIO — CHRISTINE KING

Christine King is originally from London but now lives in Sussex and has been writing professionally for over four years. Her works range from Children's books to Horror to Non-Fiction.

Christine enjoys archery, a good cocktail, and sushi. She is a wife, mother, and substitute English teacher. She also helps to run the PTA at her daughter's school and volunteers for dementia UK. People always seem surprised that she writes horror, and they say she is too nice to scare readers, which makes Christine a little worried that people don't know her very well.

You can learn more here
https://christinekingauthor.wixsite.com/mysite

JOHN, AND JOAN
BY A.J. BALL

The rain poured hard and loud that late August night; tap-dancing upon John's flat cap, and the roof of the taxi cab, as it pulled up beside him. He took the back seat and removed his sodden hat, brushing his white hair back across his balding scalp. The driver looked in his mirror at the old leather face behind him. "Where to grandad?" He asked.

"18 Lowland Road," slurred John, from his one too many gins.

As the wheels turned, leaving the noise of the 'Singing Crow Tavern' behind, the curious eyes of the driver shifted back and forth to his rear-view mirror.

John was Irritated, "go on, say it then." He mumbled to himself.

"Out a little late tonight aren't we sir?"

Oh, and there it is. John found the question frustrating; society expects that an old man, halfway into his eighties, should be home at night, with tweed slippers, and pyjamas; a woollen blanket across his lap, and teeth submerged in a glass cup next to his armchair. Catching flies after having fallen asleep, whilst some old Clark Gable picture plays for the hundredth time.

"He probably doesn't even know who Clark Gable is." John quietly remarked to himself, before raising his voice, "I was at the 'class of '65', school reunion; they built the 'Singing Crow Tavern' where our school used to be y' know... I wouldn't usually bother with reunions but...well, there's only five of us left now, thought that this may be the last chance I'll get to see them." A sad look falls upon his face as his mind projects those lost, "Tommy 'the rocket' Rickles, Charlie 'big mouth' Boxford, Simon 'speedy legs' Cooper, Jake, and Robert Miles -the Dust brothers - so many have gone. We all used to play billiards together down at Sutton Hill, there was a club there, we used to..." John looks to the driver who's clearly not listening anymore, if he ever was. "Tut,

tut," Just another old codger rambling on about the good old virile days.

The whooshing sound of a car passed by at high speed, pursued by 'the law' playing the usual police soundtrack, blaring its siren with flashing blue lights that invaded John's tired eyes. "He'll never sell ice creams going at that speed" joked John, his attempt at levity a failure as the driver remained silent.

With a yawn, John started to think of bed, thinking of how glad he'd be to get home that night, tweed slippers, pyjamas, and a sleeping mask across his sore eyes. Yes sir, John couldn't wait.

The taxi pulled up beside his home, the screech of the taxi's brakes woke him from slumber. Must have nodded off. John looked through the rain-soaked window to get his bearings, when a lightning strike illuminated the silhouette of his home, the time on his watch revealed he was home ten minutes earlier than expected.

He grabbed his flat cap and reached inside his coat pocket for his leather wallet, surprisingly, the driver told him, "no charge." John didn't argue, pleased to save himself some money. Appreciatively, John thanked the driver. "Bless you, son." And stepped out into the rain.

He pulled up his collar and tucked in his chin as he proceeded to walk to his house, quickening the pace to avoid the heavy downpour as much as he could.

Inside his home he greeted the snoring terrier, snoozing on his coat, "Hello Prince."

A half-batted eyelid and a touch of flatulence came the reply to his master. John quietly grumbled in disgust. Knowing that his wife, Joan would be fast asleep, John carefully crept up the stairs as if he were trying not to wake a sleeping dragon; but creaking steps and creaking knees were seemingly trying to betray him. At least he felt sobered up.

Sweet success, standing at the top of the wooden hill feeling like Rocky, he knew all that was left to do, was to shed his clothes and slide into the finish line.

But then his heart sank, and his stomach rumbled with dread: His wife was awake, but she was crying,

Crying? He recalled that her sister was ill, and he feared the worst.

Sitting on her bed sobbing, and clutching a framed photograph, pressing it to her chest, Joan called for her husband.

"I'm right here, Petal." He always called her that: his pretty rose petal. A little wilted now perhaps, but still the apple of his eye.

She pulled away the photograph from her breast, taking one last look before placing it on the bedside table, and slipping into bed, now soaking the pillow in heartache's rain.

The photograph caught his eye; it wasn't her sister that she wept for... it was John.

Through the window, a blasting beam of light shone through. It wasn't a heavenly light, but the taxi cab now stationary in front of his home. Its horn sounded, beckoning him back inside.

In shock, and confusion, John stared at the bedroom wall adorned with family images of those lost through the years: His brother Charlton, lost to cancer, his sister Beryl passed due to old age, mother Susan, and father William, both departed too from old age, and his son David, the most tragic loss of all. David died at the young age of 29, due to a complication occurring during heart surgery ...and now himself? John knew his picture wasn't on the wall, but perhaps it was soon to join the others.

"No, this is ludicrous," he said with defiance as he reached to take hold of his wife for assurance. Assurance that he was still amongst the living. Suddenly he found himself back outside, staring down the bright headlights of the taxi cab that he took to get here. He cautiously approached the front of the vehicle; the dark windscreen of the cab concealed the face behind the glass. Then all at once, the back door swung invitingly open. "What's going on?!" John shouted.

The driver's door opened, and the driver stepped out. "Hello Dad, it's time to go."

John's voice trembled in reply, "David?"

His dead son stood before him, but the picture of good health, just like he was before he passed.

"If you haven't figured it out already Dad, let me spell it out for you... you're dead!"

"Piss off, I'm bloody dreaming."

"No Dad, it's no dream...look at your watch, it hasn't moved since ten to midnight on August 27th. Today is the 30th." John's blank expression said it all. "You got into the taxi with a middle-aged driver, you left it with me driving. No charge, remember?"

"I thought the driver had changed, but ...but, I thought it was the drink! That was you?"

"Not drunk anymore, are you Dad? And how are your clothes, huh? Dry? What about that coat, the dog was asleep on that very coat, didn't you notice?"

"How did I ..."

"The police car that passed was chasing a car that overturned, and your taxi was involved in a collision. I've brought you home to say goodbye, Dad." John stood there shaking his head in disbelief.

"But your mother called me."

"She did, but you were not really there, you're not really here Dad; think of it like you're looking through a window, you're inside, and all of this is outside. I'm sorry for smiling Dad, but it's great to see you again".

"You too son, it's...it's just I don't want to leave your mother's side".

"It won't be for long, Dad; I'll bring you back to see her again, I promise; everybody's waiting to see you, come on." John took a last, long look at his house before stepping into the back of the taxi, but instead of sitting down in the cab's backseat, he found himself sitting at the counter of his father's bar. "My God, they tore this down years ago, asbestos they said." John looked around, amazed at how it all looked just as he remembered it. Even the smell of the flowers from the vase was so familiar, "Lavender. Is this real?" He asked.

"This is your father's bar...time is not quite as in charge here Dad, we could go as far back as to witness your birth if you like?"

"Oh, bloody hell, no. Hey, can I have a Guinness?"

"Sure, wouldn't be heaven otherwise." Smirked David, who walked around to pour the pint.

John wondered how a stout would taste after death. He took a large gulp, and with a satisfied look on his face, and a lip of froth, he gave his vote, "exceptional."

But things were missing; the people, the smell of spilt beer, and cider, cigarette smoke legally wafting through the air, the noise of laughter, and the clinking of glass. No, the bar was too quiet.

David asked his father to turn around and look behind him.

If John's heart was still beating it may have stopped, in that moment. There at a large, round table, his family sat smiling at him. His brother, father, mother, aunts, uncles, gran, and grandpa. All those that had passed were now sitting right there in front of him. A tear threatened to fall down his cheek as he joined his family in a heartfelt cheer, with glasses raised in his honour.

It felt like a whole day passed as they exchanged stories, and memories; John was so happy, but something was still missing... rather someone was missing.

David asked his father, "would you like to go back, and see Mum now, Dad?"

"Yes." John looked at all the faces as they faded away into a hue of heavenly white.

"You'll see them again soon, Dad."

John then found himself back inside his bedroom, his wife was still in bed where he had left her.

"Pet, I just want you to know how very much I love you. You came to me in a time of my life when I really wasn't sure about a lot of things, about life, and about myself. But you gave me the courage, and the belief to live in happiness." John's tears fell as he struggled to speak. Knowing what he had to say next,

David softly interjected: "She can hear you now Dad, but don't say goodbye... Try hello instead. Time is not quite as in charge here, remember."

David faded away from sight, as a voice called to John.

Man and wife, reunited, they fade hand in hand into that heavenly white.

AUTHOR BIO — ANTHONY J BALL

Anthony J Ball is a new poet, writer, and author from the West Midlands.
'Asleep at 3 AM', his first book was released on May the 3rd 2020.
He is the Winner of the T.B.M Christmas Terror competition 2019; and so far published in, 'The Last Time' - Lucy Onions, Black Dream 2020, Poetic Vision by Dream Well, and the Stafford Space Station Spring, Summer, and Autumn PoeTree project collections.

FATHER KNOWS BEST
BY KEVIN SHAW

"Mornin love, where's it to?" the driver asked.

A Northern Irishman. Mary hesitated and almost got back out.

'I am not getting into a discussion about religion with a black cab driver, especially today,' she thought.

"Not sure where you are going to love?" he smiled, "I can take you for a ride around and back here for twenty quid if you like?"

"Sorry, yes, the carpet shop in the old bingo hall, near East Ham Station, please." It was a mile from St Joseph's Church, but the only place nearby she could think of.

They arrived at The East Ham Carpet Warehouse, and she stepped out. The black cab driver didn't head off immediately, so she felt obliged to go in and pretended to browse carpets until he left.

The walk was closer to two miles but did give her the opportunity to get her thoughts together. Mary was now glad to have put on her long coat, although her original reason was misplaced guilt about "adorning oneself modestly" when in church.

Walking down the side of St Joseph's Church, a gust of wind whipped up the early autumn leaves from the gutter. Memories whirled like the suddenly animated leaves. Recollections of Grandma, church, Sunday dinner, and family.

"Don't be forgetful English-Born children," her Grandma used to say when eulogizing Ireland, even though she had never been there herself. "We are here in this God-forsaken country for a reason. On his way to England as a boy, your Great-Grandfather... (at this point everyone in the family would groan)... fell off the deck of the ship, but an angel sent by God in the form of a man grabbed his ankle as he went over. It was God's hand, and without that divine intervention none of ye would exist." One Christmas they began to count every retelling of the story, arriving at thirty-three by Easter.

One lucky grab of an ankle rescues generations, Mary thought. Why doesn't God always rescue?

"Don't question! Father knows best!" the nuns would shriek.

The brick-built church was unremarkable in design, it being one of the places of worship hastily erected to accommodate immigrant Catholics a century earlier. A poorly executed graffiti tag adorned the Church door like a not-so-ancient curse. Mary paused there for several moments, her heart pounding as she pushed down on the handle and went in. The temperature inside was barely above the autumnal outside, the brick walls and pillars radiating cold.

Mass was concluding, the air heavy with incense as a sombre post-communion group of elderly people crossed themselves for the blessing and dismissal. The Mass is ended. The smells and sounds swarmed in Mary's senses. Comfort and rage.

The congregation greeted one other and passed out of the Church, with most offering Mary a nod or a smile. One of the ladies helping clear up at the front spotted her and limped briskly down the aisle. Her confidence with the limp said it was something she had lived with for a long time.

"Hello love, can I help?" the lady asked.

Mary felt her neck reddening.

"I'm here to see Father James, he is expecting me. It's Mary."

"Ok, take a pew and I'll let him know you are here. He's just in the sacristy taking off his dress." The lady smirked and winked, before turning and limping efficiently away.

As she waited, Mary browsed nervously around the empty church, stopping at the parish notice board at the back. There were posters for concerts, charity shops, world missions, and wedding photographers. There was also a poster for the Prison Visitors Scheme:

"Why not become a Prison Visitor? For the Lord, Himself said. "Come you who are blessed by My Father… for I was in prison and you visited me."

She rested her fingertips on the table, trying to contain her nausea.

"Mary, is it?"

She jumped; Father James having appeared silently behind her.

He apologized and held out his hand. It was dry and smooth; Mary's was clammy and burning. Father James was probably in his early seventies, with multi-toned grey hair and the slender look of a man who lived simply. His smile was warm and broad, his eyes dark and alert.

Mary forced a smile, a little girl again.

"Thank you for seeing me Father, especially at such short notice."

She could see he was trying to read her as if there were only a few stories a young woman might be.

"Shall we head over to the Community Centre?" he suggested, "they have a tea dance at eleven and we'll be able to get tea and cake before the grab-a-granny crew arrive."

Mary laughed, realising she had been holding her breath. She felt a wave of relief, both at the rush of oxygen and his friendly manner. This was also something to worry about, him being a Priest who put sinners at ease.

They sat by a large window looking out onto the car park, each sipping weak tea. The Community Centre was a busy hub of slightly outdated activities, from the tea dance to a jumble sale, to the Mother and Toddlers group and a Church Youth club. The centre's 70s décor was in desperate need of updating, although the smell of stale cigarette smoke and alcohol was oddly comforting to Mary. The aroma of Girl Guides and Christmas parties.

"So, Mary," Father James ventured, "you said on the phone there was something you wanted to discuss with me?"

Mary drew a deep inner breath.

"Well, Father, it's about my daughter, but me also, I suppose. You see, things happened to both of us. Me when I was a little girl, and then, sadly, my daughter."

Mary paused; the rest of the story having stuck somewhere in her chest. She looked out of the window and across to a row of tall conifers that stood along the edge of the car park. An elderly man was cutting the grass beneath them.

Father James looked intently at Mary, his face not indicating any view or judgment. He stared into his tea momentarily, before looking back up with an expression that said he understood. Mary imagined him thinking, "Oh, she's that story."

After a few more moments of silence, he said, "Mary, I'm guessing that what happened to you was in the Church, but your precious little one was elsewhere? You probably also feel guilt that having been through this yourself, you should have headed off the risks for your daughter?"

He looked at her without any smugness at this understanding, like he wished he didn't have it. His eyes were glassy.

"That's exactly right Father," Mary nodded, without looking up.

After more silence, she told him what had happened.

One of the Priests at her convent school had sifted her out, using all kinds of excuses to get her to his study at lunchtimes and in the evening. The nuns should have been a refuge, but they were not. 'Father knows best' was their answer to everything. Her daughter had been abused at the age of 11 by a friend's dad.

Fortunately, she had found the courage to tell her Mum immediately, but the damage was done. He went to prison, having done it before, but no system or person had warned Mary. Not the Police, not his wife, not her own instincts.

"All too familiar a story, I suppose," Mary said.

"It's heartbreakingly familiar," Father James said, "but never ordinary. Your hurt is yours, and it isn't made easier by being common."

He looked down into his mug, wondering if there was any more to be said, or if this was going to lead to Police involvement.

"Is this your first time coming back to Church for something other than a wedding or funeral?" Father James asked, appearing genuinely interested rather than judgmental.

Mary nodded, looking back out at the conifers. They were usually planted to hide something, in this case, the council waste centre.

"I'm not here to ask you to do anything Father. I'm actually here about your prison work."

At this, Father James woke from his relaxed listening state, the conversation having taken an unexpected turn.

"You are Chaplain to HMP Blinley, are you not?" She asked.

"I am," he said, looking puzzled, "are you interested in that work?"

"Interested?" Mary laughed out loud, "not exactly."

Standing suddenly, Mary said, "Can we go back to the church for me to make confession please Father?"

Shocked by the request, Father James jumped straight up and knocked over the remainder of his tea. He followed Mary out as one of the tea dance helpers came over with a dishcloth.

Sitting in the confessional, Mary folded her arms across her stomach and leant forward. The smell of wood and brass polish turned the small booth into a time machine. Joy and pain.

As a girl, she had racked her brains for sins to confess, and like most of her friends, she made things up. There were non-existent kissed boys, lots of bad thoughts, and even a stolen car (dreamt up after watching Bonnie and Clyde). She remembered hearing the Priest stifle a laugh when she confessed this. Soon enough she had some real sins to confess but couldn't speak them out loud. It took years to understand they were not her sins, and many more years to actually feel that they were not her sins.

Father James coughed from his side of the partition, bringing her back to the present.

"Can I ask something before I make confession Father?" Mary asked.

"Go ahead my child," he responded sombrely, having a formal voice for this part of his job.

"Do you offer the prisoners forgiveness and absolution Father?"

"I do, according to the teaching of the Church."

"Do you ever think they don't deserve it?"

Father James hesitated before speaking.

"Well, it is not ours to judge. God offers forgiveness in response to repentance, not I."

"Have you ever wondered if God is wrong to offer forgiveness?" Mary asked.

He was silent for a few more moments.

"Mary, I understand your line of reasoning, but it is a dead-end road. God is sovereign and men's lives rest in his hand, not ours."

"What about women's lives, whose hand do they rest in?" Mary asked.

'Father knows best!' echoed in her ears.

More silence.

Mary spoke again.

"Father, the man who was killed on the day of his release from your prison last month, he is the man who molested my daughter."

Mary heard his bench creak as he sat up. After a pause, he spoke.

"I cannot speak of specific cases in regard to my prison work Mary."

"Did you or any other Priest ever offer him absolution, Father?"

The silence from the other side of the screen told Mary she was not going to get an answer. A full minute passed.

"Father forgive me for I have sinned. It has been twenty-three years since my last confession."

She heard the creak of wood again.

"Go ahead my child," he said gently.

"I have harboured a bitterness that has always pushed away those who love me. My mistrust of everything and everyone means I have consistently hurt those who are closest."

Sunlight glinted through the crack in the confessional door, illuminating fine dust particles in the air. Her heart began to race.

"Forgive me Father. I had him killed. To protect my daughter, I arranged for him to be killed. I am yet to arrive at regret and full repentance for my actions. For this, I seek God's help and mercy."

Father James was deathly silent. This was not a normal day at the office now. A pause of what felt like several minutes elapsed. Eventually, he spoke.

"Mary, Seeking God's forgiveness is a big step on the road to freedom, but there may be more you need to do. I am bound by confessional seal to hold within me forever what you have admitted but search your own heart, Mary. Are you able to live with this burden?"

They remained in silence for a long time.

Father James sighed heavily and spoke softly.

"Mary, I would like to invite you into the fold of St Joseph's. You are welcome here at Mass my daughter, and you will always have my ear. I offer you and your daughter a refuge, a place of safety and peace. We will walk together and see where God leads."

Father James carefully offered a range of penitent prayers, just as Mary had experienced in her youth. This time, however, she was guilty.

She thanked Father James, but as she stood to leave, he spoke in a voice that was barely a whisper.

"Mary. He that you speak of never presented himself at Mass. He was unknown to the Chapel and all Chaplains."

They held silence together again.

Mary stepped out into the church, and then out into the light.

Father knows best.

AUTHOR BIO — KEVIN SHAW

Kevin Shaw has had a varied working life, including many years spent at BMW, Mercedes, and Ferrari. He has also worked as Probation Staff in prisons and is currently a Mental Health Chaplain in the NHS, specialising in Forensic Environments.

As a writer, he has won several short story awards and regularly writes for faith and spirituality focused publications.

He has just completed his first novel and is seeking an agent.

In his spare time, Kevin enjoys family, running, cycling, and playing double bass on the local Jazz scene.

EARLY MORNING RAIN
BY L. STEPHENSON

Tony couldn't help but think about the fight he had with Danny earlier that night as he pressed his forehead against the window of the black cab.

The outside world may as well have not existed as it rushed by his glassy gaze. All he could see was the look that his brother gave him. The sheer sadness planted a dry lump in his throat. He was as guilty as he was strangely relieved that he could still hurt him like that.

The cab shook as it grazed a pothole in the road, shaking Tony from his early morning daze.

"Turn left here, please." He told the driver. "Cheers."

He saw his brother's car the moment they rounded the corner onto his street. No one seemed to be driving it as it free rolled backwards across the road.

Tony opened the cab door as they were still moving as he called out. He could see his brother sitting unconscious in the driver's seat. Leaping out of the cab, he started to run as fast as he could the very second he spotted the blood.

* * *

4 hours earlier...

"Mum's worried about you," Tony said as he finished rolling his joint.

Just 23 years old; his eyebrows were thick and brown beneath a headful of fluffy blonde hair. He could be mistaken for being devastatingly handsome if he didn't always dress like such a slacker. Nevertheless, despite this contradiction of appearances, he emanated an infectious adorability that often sparked jealousy amongst his other male peers.

He and his brother, Danny, sat backstage as the silver-painted walls around them boomed with the bass reverberating through the club. He slouched on a shiny, faux-leather sofa behind Danny, who occupied one of the four dressing room mirrors.

Danny was a strange beast. He had all the trappings of an aging hipster while carrying with him the paradoxical belief that he was, in fact, too cool to be an aging hipster.

Tony couldn't decide what pissed him off more, his brother's hypocrisy, or the way he was looking him up and down with disapproval.

"She's worried about me?" Danny frowned at the paper balancing between his younger sibling's fingers.

Tony giggled as he flicked away at his lighter. "She knows what I'm about."

As he looked around the spacious room they were in, he couldn't help but notice how bare it was, save for Danny's drink of choice and a couple of glasses.

"Not exactly the red-carpet treatment." He remarked. "Aren't you supposed to be their headliner?"

"All weekend." Danny sighed, slumping in his disinterest.

"I thought you guys were supposed to have entourages, and groupies, and stuff."

"So what? The concern is that I'm not doing the drugs, and the lasses, and all the excessive crap?" The older of the two was now more annoyed than perplexed, shaking his head as he checked the time on his phone.

"It's just you, Danny boy." Giving up on his lighter, Tony pocketed it along with his weed for later. "That's the point. Where is everybody? Don't you have any mates?"

Danny didn't answer.

"You can't go through life alone. It's not good for a man's soul."

"Quit it." Danny snapped. "You're starting to sound like dad."

"At least one of us does."

Danny shot his brother a look so fast the chair beneath him creaked. His eyes burned into him.

A few moments of cutting silence had passed by when he looked away and said, "Get out…"

After his set was over, Danny stopped at a gas station on his way home to buy beer, some potato chips, and a candy bar. True to form, he spoke to no one. Not even the attendant, nor the cashier.

A handful of partygoers recognised and waved to him as he climbed back into his work van. He ignored them, too.

He watched the houses of the people that lived on his street go by. He didn't know them, and they didn't know him. Was that really so wrong?

Pulling into his driveway, he opened the van door and hopped down, paper bag underarm. He turned around and…

…there was a flash. A tiny explosion.

The paper bag burst open as it hit the ground.

Danny's hands shook as he struggled to pull up his shirt. It clung tightly to his skin, soaked with the blood seeping from the bullet hole in his stomach.

Smoke rose into the early morning air from the muzzle of the gun that was still pointed at him. The lad holding the weapon creased his brow as he pulled the trigger a second time.

This one caught Danny in the shoulder, slamming him back against the side of his van.

90

The lad's accomplice screamed something from somewhere inside the vehicle. He couldn't tell what it was.

Sound had become the echo of an echo, fading further and further away. Followed by sight as the lad with the gun seemed to vanish into thin air. And last of all touch, as he was numb to the vibration of the van as it rumbled and rattled to life. Nor did he feel the side mirror that struck him in the ear.

Danny saw the world fall on its side. Blood pooled out from him on the driveway as the van backed out onto the road, tyres shrieking as it sped away.

The houses across the street became a dizzying blur to Danny's vision as he lay there on the cold concrete waiting for help to come. But the pavement was silent. Gradually, his ears became dimly aware of the rain that fell softly down upon his body.

Finally, his eyes found the cracked glass of the side mirror lying mere inches away from his face before they fluttered and closed.

Where was he?

It was like floating inside a darkness that simultaneously passed through him just as much as it surrounded him.

The pitter-patter of the rain was like gentle white noise. Waves of faintly drumming static. And it was getting louder.

Sound was returning.

His eyes snapped wide open with a shrill gasp. He coughed out the raindrops that had fallen down the wrong side of his throat. As he focused on his reflection, his shoulder and stomach began to throb. He opened and closed his fingers. He kicked his feet.

Trembling with a dull agony, Danny rolled over and rose to his hands and knees. Minding his wounded shoulder, a watery trail of blood droplets was left by his stomach as he crawled up the driveway towards his car.

A set of keys jangled as they fell from his pants pocket. Scooping them up with a pained grunt, he pierced one through the keyhole of a door. The car shook as he lost his balance, collapsing against the smooth aluminium.

Punching the frame, Danny wept in his frustration as his fingers weakly fought the handle. Eventually, there was a click as the door jerked open.

With the strength of his good arm and two legs of jelly, the rubber grip on the steering wheel groaned as Danny dragged himself up into the driver's seat, screaming through clenched teeth as he went.

The right side of his body ached beneath his injury as he stopped to catch his breath. His shoulders rose and fell, rose and fell, rose, and fell. Each breath became longer and longer. And quieter and quieter. His eyes stared blindly ahead at the foggy windscreen. Ever so soundly, his mouth dropped open and his head rolled back as that enveloping darkness grasped him once again.

Wholly unaware he had used it as an anchor for his waning consciousness, his heavy knuckles ground the parking brake downward until it relented. There was a blunt pop, accompanied by a jolt before Danny's car started rolling down the driveway. It bounced backwards off the sidewalk and into the road.

"Danny…?" A voice called from the street.

The car backed into a neighbour's motor home. Without a fastened belt to secure him, the impact threw Danny's limp body forward. His mouth bumped off the top of the steering wheel before he collapsed on his side.

"Christ! Danny!" The voice belonged to Tony as he raced from a black cab. Yanking the passenger door open, he crumpled at the sight of his brother. "Danny…My God, Danny, what happened to you?"

Tony's hands trembled uncontrollably as they followed the bloodstains, hovering from one bullet wound to the other. His fingers traced the body for any further signs of harm.

"Who did this to you, mate?" He whimpered, choking back tears. "I'm gonna kill 'em."

He flinched at the sound of the cab zooming back up the street in reverse. Tony was pretty sure that he wasn't coming back. He shot the driver a single glare.

"What the…" Words failed him for a moment in his disgust and astonishment. "Selfish pillock…"

Turning back to his brother, he hesitated before he wrapped his arms under Danny's shoulders.

"I know this is gonna hurt, mate." He said softly to him. "But I gotta move you. Otherwise, I can't take you anywhere. Okay? Here we go."

Tony strained as he pulled and kept pulling until Danny was upright and belted fast into the passenger's seat. He ran around to the driver's side where the keys were still stuck in the door. He retrieved the set from their keyhole and climbed in.

Just as he started the car, a stocky fellow appeared in a stripy night-shirt and dark dressing gown. His beady-eyed face was lobster red beneath a thinning tuft of ginger hair as he pounded on the car window.

"Where do you think you're going?" He barked as Tony rolled down the glass. "He just smashed into my motor home. I spent a huge piece of my early retirement on that. You're not going anywhere, sonny."

"Are you taking the mick?!" Tony screamed back. "I can see my brother's blood on the bloody ground! And you're worried about a piece of rolling metal…"

The neighbour said no more as Tony slowly turned the car.

"To hell with you and your sodding motor home." He sneered at the man before he sped away.

As they turned out onto the main road, Tony rolled down the windows, hoping that the icy burst might bring Danny round. The rain had stopped a few minutes ago, so Tony could just about hear the laughter of club-goers on their way back to their hotels over the hum of the road and the wind rushing through the car. Danny, however, did not stir.

Luckily, it was early enough in the morning for there to be little to no traffic on the road. If he could maintain their current speed for just a little while longer, they would be at the hospital in no time.

To calm his nerves, Tony turned on the radio to distract himself. After a seemingly endless selection of rock, easy listening, and jazz, at last he landed upon a sports channel. It was a live broadcast. The game was already over, and the winning team's celebrations were just beginning. The car speakers erupted with the sound of countless fireworks. Hundreds and thousands of pops and bangs.

As Tony watched the road, he failed to realise his brother had awoken. Failed to see the panic and the tears. Danny had no idea where he was, what was happening, or who he was with, and he was terrified. He let out a frenzied cry. And in a moment of pure delirium, he saw the lad with the gun sitting next to him in the driver's seat. So, he lunged at him.

The car veered over to the edge, sparks flying as it shredded through the barrier. For a single breath, it left the ground. But as gravity brought it back down again, it clipped the road, sending it into a rapid tumble-drop over the side.

Danny didn't make a sound. Despite his little brother's screams, he watched silently as the world spun them to their insignificant little deaths.

* * *

Danny's work van ground to a halt in an alleyway as the rain fell. It shook and jumped as the getaway driver backed his way out of the vehicle and onto the wet concrete.

"You shot him!" He scolded the lad. "I can't believe you bloody shot him!"

"Because you told me to!" The boy's squeaky, little voice replied from the passenger's seat.

"I've got to get back there." Tony turned away from the van as he pulled off his balaclava and dropped it onto a flooding drain. "I just wanted to scare him. Make him see."

"Where are you going?"

He ignored the lad as he jogged out of the alley and onto the street. As the early morning rain cooled the sweat of a guilty man on his brow, he hailed the first black cab that came his way.

AUTHOR BIO — L. STEPHENSON

I studied Film & TV Screenwriting at UCLAN, graduating with Honours. Since then I have been fortunate to be featured in 5 anthologies. Ghosts, Goblins, Murder & Madness, Stuff of Nightmares, Shadowy Natures, Unburied, an LGBT related set also releasing this year, and the one you are reading now. I have also completed my first novella.

PUBLISHERS NOTE

CAAB Publishing would like to thank all of the contributors to this anthology, we received a high quality of submissions and unfortunately not everyone could be included but we thank you all for your efforts.

ABOUT THE PUBLISHERS

CAAB Publishing is a traditional indie publishing company.

At C.A.A.B Publishing we are committed to supporting our authors and helping them promote their work to the widest market possible.

Through hard work and networking, we want to make all our authors successful and give as many writers as possible that wonderful moment when you read, "We loved your work, and we want to publish it."

We want to create a true partnership approach to promoting your books.

We strive towards building a supportive network of authors. We expect every author to publicise themselves and promote their books alongside our own promotional activity.

We will always be inspiring writers and supporting authors.

www.caabpublishing.co.uk

Other books available from CAAB Publishing

SURVIVING THE RAVENOUS

Cathy is on the road trip from hell.

She has woken up after a global attack, her life has been devastated but she is still alive. Where there is life, there is hope...isn't there?

In a world full of unknown terror. Cathy finds a group of young people trying to survive and looking for some normality in a world of fear.

Stalked by mindless, killing machines that used to be their friends and neighbors and surrounded by death, they try to get to a sanctuary that may not exist. They discover that other people can be more deadly than the creatures chasing them, and things are not always what they seem.

Cathy has no idea if it is worth going on. Can she navigate these new friendships, her feelings, and be strong enough to find the thing she craves the most.

Hope.

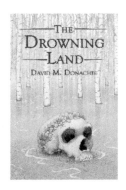

THE WORLD IS DROWNING

Edan's tribe has always survived by knowing the land and following its stories. But now their world is changing, and they must change with it, or die. When young fisherman Edan rescues the troll seer Tara from Phelan wolf-touched, he makes a powerful enemy. But Tara's visions bring them hope that the world might still be saved.

Edan must break away from tradition and cross the Summer Lands in search of a new future, but where does that future lie? With Phelan's wolf clan? With the Fomor sea-devils? Or with Tara's uncertain hope for salvation?

The Drowning Land takes us back eight thousand years to the Mesolithic Period when a lost land, Doggerland, still connected England to France across what is now the North Sea.

Inspired by the extensive research conducted by archaeologists over the past two decades, this is a story of our distant ancestors and how they confronted the climate catastrophe that overwhelmed their world.

Available at www.caabpublishing.co.uk Amazon and Other leading retailers.

Printed in Great Britain
by Amazon

25070139R00056